BROKEN MATE

SHADOW CITY: SILVER WOLF

JEN L. GREY

CHAPTER ONE

A scream echoed in my ears, making my blood run cold. The noise originated from about two miles away, where my pack lived, deep within the mountainous woods outside of Chattanooga, Tennessee.

I stilled. *That was odd.* The trickling of the murky Tennessee River in front of me filtered back into my awareness.

Maybe some kids were playing or Dad was doing training rituals with the younger shifters. But that would surprise me because tonight was the new moon. Normally, we took it easy this day of the month when our kind was at our weakest—but maybe that was the point.

I hoped no one had gotten hurt.

Brushing the concern away, I leaned over the muddy edge of the riverbank and dipped my fingers into the cool water. The heavy storm from a few days ago had made the liquid more cloudy than normal, but I could still see my reflection. My long, silver hair, which signified my future as alpha, lifted in the breeze, and the olive tint to my skin contrasted with my light silver-purple eyes.

The noon sun warmed the back of my neck, and the tension melted from my body.

"Attack!" The faint, desperate command resonated from the distance. "Kill as many as you can."

My body froze.

This was no exercise. We didn't shout frantically even when we wanted to during training. Revealing worry sounded weak. As silver wolves and protectors, we had to convey confidence at all times.

I spun on my heel and ran toward the neighborhood. Dammit, I shouldn't have snuck out and hiked the two miles away from home, but this was the one day of the month that I could be alone for a few hours.

The one day I had a reprieve from learning about my future responsibilities, which I'd inherit from my father.

What's going on? I linked with my pack, but there was radio silence. As though I'd been cut off from communicating with them.

That had never happened before. I probed my mind again for the link while panic clawed in my throat. The only solace I had was that my chest was still warm from my pack bonds.

Animals scurried in the opposite direction as me, and my already frantic heart pounded harder.

Something was wrong. The silver wolves acclimated into the world, but we kept our location and the type of wolf we were hidden from everyone, including other members of the wolf race. The only time we allowed someone from outside into our pack was when one of our own found their fated mate. To keep our pack secret, the fated mate always became one of us. It was our pack law and a way to ensure that the silver wolf race remained hidden. So, being attacked shouldn't have been possible.

Gunshots fired, and I drew magic from my wolf, increasing my speed with the animal inside. I needed to get back to my pack as fast as possible, but I couldn't risk shifting. In animal form, we revealed the kind of wolves we were to our attackers, our silver fur unmistakable. I couldn't take the risk of alerting them to our existence, in case they thought we were another regular wolf pack. The attackers could be from a pack led by an overzealous alpha who wanted to form a larger pack by strong-arming us into submitting to him. Dad had told me repeatedly that something like this could happen.

It was a possibility, but I couldn't be sure until I reached them.

Parts of my chest grew colder as members of the pack began to disappear, just like the time my grandfather passed.

No.

They couldn't be dying.

Any other day of the month, I could run twice as fast, but with the moon hidden tonight, my magic was weakened even more so than the other pack members' would be because alpha blood was more connected to the moon. Even in wolf form, I wouldn't have been able to run faster.

Not today.

Silver wolves were much stronger than standard wolves, especially at night and on a full moon. The fuller the moon, the stronger and larger we were. But this one day of the month, we were essentially like every other wolf in the world.

Nothing special.

More shots blasted, and I pushed myself harder, causing my side to cramp.

I had to breathe, or I'd be too winded to help my pack when I finally reached them.

The trees blurred as I rushed past, and my feet sank into the mulch-like ground, slowing me down. I wanted to scream in frustration.

Taking deep breaths of the spring air, I tried to use the floral scents of the woods to keep myself rational. Deep breathing was one of the calming rituals that had been instilled in me as a young girl. Learning airway control was one of the best weapons that anyone could have. It helped me think rationally and not make stupid decisions under pressure. Nothing was more powerful.

No matter how hard I pushed, it didn't seem to be enough. It felt like time stood still as I desperately tried to get to my friends and family.

With every step I took, the sounds of fighting became clearer. I had to believe that was a good sign. After all, we were born warriors.

I latched on to that hope and didn't let my fear take hold.

As the trees thinned, I almost shouted in victory. *I made it!* But the stench of copper hit my nose.

Blood.

The smell coated my throat, making it hard to swallow.

My feet stumbled, and I caught myself before I could fall to my knees. I didn't have time to come apart. I was an alpha, for God's sake, and my people needed me.

I opened my mouth and breathed without using my nose. The scent was still strong, but not nearly as bad. My wolf surged forward in my mind, helping me to remain emotionally strong.

As I got closer to home, modest brick houses peeked through the trees. I ran directly to the alpha house, its backyard connected to the woods. I had to find my parents and see what Dad needed me to do. He'd have a plan. He always did.

Needing to be as silent as possible, I slowed, not wanting to stumble upon an attacker. It wasn't as if they would be broadcasting their location to me.

The fighting sounded like a drum pounding.

Overwhelming.

Devastating.

Heartbreaking.

When I came close to breaking through the trees, an unfamiliar musky stench almost made me gag, stopping me in my tracks.

The attackers were definitely wolf shifters, but I didn't know their scents.

I squatted and removed the knife that I kept holstered around my ankle. Having it brought me comfort, and I never left the house without the weapon. Not even when Zoe, my best friend, gave me shit, asking what kind of critter would be brave enough to attack us.

I bet she'd changed her tune now.

"The girl has to be here somewhere," a male whispered. "I think I've found her scent heading into the woods."

"Maybe she ran," someone with a deeper voice responded. "The alpha, Arian, may have told her to leave."

I peeked from around a tree and saw two men dressed in all black and wearing ski masks, standing in my backyard. They were both over six feet tall, like Dad, and were muscled and stout, even more than most shifters. Whoever these assholes were, they worked out a lot, which alarmed me. That could mean they'd been training intensely for something.

A shiver ran down my spine as I realized they might know what we were.

But again, that shouldn't be possible. Everyone outside of our pack thought our kind had died off. Still... they knew my dad's name.

Breathe, Sterlyn. If I let my emotions get the best of me, they'd find me and do who knew what else. I clutched the hilt of the knife, holding it so I could use the blade easily if needed.

I couldn't see anyone else from this position, which aggravated me. I didn't want to shift—at least, not yet—in case they didn't know what we were. *Dad?* I tried to link to him again.

Instead of a response, more screams filled the air, sounding like they came from the front of my house. The breeze changed direction, blowing against me and toward the two pricks.

Dammit, I had to make my move fast.

"Her scent grows stronger this way." The speaker lifted his black mask, revealing an auburn goatee, and stopped it at his nose. He sniffed deeply. "She smells like freesia."

"Are you being serious?" The other guy reached over and yanked the first man's mask back down. "Freesia? What'd you do, go paint your nails with your mom before heading over here?"

My pack was being slaughtered by dumbasses who wore all black during the day and argued about scents.

The enemy didn't even feel bad about decimating my pack. What kind of heartless bastards were they? Rage coiled tightly around me, and I dug my fingernails into my free palm, making blood pool at my fingertips.

I took a few steps deeper into the woods and then moved toward them, hoping to catch them off guard.

"Don't be an asshole, Earl," Goatee scoffed. "I'm saying she smells pretty. Maybe I'll get a chance to breed with her."

Nausea rolled in my stomach. Why was he talking about breeding?

"Then say that. That's at least acceptable, and don't get your hopes up. They already have someone in mind for her." The other guy shook his head. "Stop being an idiot. I got you on this crew, and you better not make me look bad. One more stupid move, and I'll kill you myself." He headed toward me.

I crouched behind some brush. Once they got near, I'd strike at the smarter one—Earl—before going after Goatee.

Forcing myself to breathe slowly, I let calm float throughout my body.

Earl lifted his hand, signaling Goatee to stop. He stalked toward me, his yellow eyes searching the brush.

He was about ten feet away, but I needed him closer. With Goatee nearby, I needed to strike fast and hard. Taking him out on the first shot was crucial. Otherwise, it would be two on one, and I didn't like those odds.

Goatee moved gracefully beside Earl. Maybe he wasn't as stupid as I thought.

Earl glanced at his friend. "She's close—"

His distraction was all that I needed. I lunged forward and slammed the knife into Earl's chest, stabbing him in the heart.

"What—" His words garbled as he snapped his head back toward me. His eyes widened, and he looked at his chest, blood already soaking his shirt.

"Shit!" Goatee screeched.

I wrapped my hands around the hilt of the knife and pulled back hard. A sickening sucking followed by a crackle sounded before the knife slid from his chest.

Blood gushed as Earl pressed his hands to the wound, trying to stop the bleeding.

Walking past him, I readied the knife in my hand as Goatee charged.

"You bitch," he growled and reached for my throat.

I dodged him and straightened, slamming my elbow into the back of his head. He fell to his knees, and I grabbed the material and hair at the back of his head.

"You're going to pay," he growled.

Irrational anger. Perfect. That meant I had the upper hand.

He jumped to his feet and snatched my hair.

Dammit, I should've pulled it up. I jerked my head away, but he held tight and yanked me toward him.

Fighting dirty it would be.

I pretended to trip and fall toward him. He leaned forward, his chest helping to steady me, and spread his legs apart.

As my shoulders connected with him, I lifted my leg, kneeing the asshole right in the balls. I didn't feel much of anything, but he released his hold and grabbed his family jewels like he actually had some.

Interesting. Either way, my plan had worked.

I punched him, and he tipped over, landing face first. Unable to bring myself to kill the asswipe now that he was the only one left, I kicked him in the head, knocking him out.

I surveyed the area, anticipating another attack, but all I could see was the man I'd killed moments ago. Hysteria clawed inside me at what I'd done.

We trained to fight, but I'd never killed anyone. I'd prayed every night that I would never have to. Obviously, my prayers hadn't been answered.

"Sterlyn!" Dad called.

His comforting voice snapped me back to the present. I turned to face him...and almost wished I hadn't.

Blood stained his white shirt, and he clutched his side, grimacing with every move he made toward me. "You need to go *now*." His normally silver eyes looked more like steel, and his hair appeared a tarnished gray. The handsome man that I'd seen earlier today looked old.

"What?" I jogged toward him, not wanting him to hurt himself more. "No. I need to help protect our pack."

"Look." He reached out a hand slicked with blood. "They're here for you, and I can't let them take you."

"For me?" My brain fogged. "Why?"

"I think they want to force you into a mate bond." He glanced over his shoulder.

My gaze followed his...and my world crashed around me. I couldn't breathe as I tried to make sense of what I saw.

Bodies littered the ground. All from my pack.

Dad and I used the thick trees of the forest to hide us over a hundred yards away as my best friend Zoe army-crawled across the road onto the grass, trying to get out of the way of the attackers. Blood poured down her arms, and I could tell she was using all of her strength to survive.

A man dressed in black ran to her and placed a gun to her temple.

I have to stop him. I moved to intervene, but warm, strong hands wrapped around my waist and pulled me backward. Dad placed his hands on my shoulders and got in my face.

The loud blast of the gun made my stomach revolt.

The spicy scent of fear wafted from Dad as he jerked. "Sterlyn, focus on me."

"But—" I pushed against his arms. *I have to save them.*

He groaned in pain. "Those men have no intention of letting any of us live except you. There are too many for us to fight off. Most of the pack connections are now cold. Almost everyone is dead."

"What?" My body froze. "Mom?"

"Yes, and I'll be following soon." He nodded toward his side.

Now that he wasn't holding it, I could see his wound. The gash was so deep that the muscle was visible, and the way the blood was pouring from it, I knew they had to have hit a main artery. Even with shifter healing, no one could survive that. "No. I'll take you to the hospital."

"I'm barely hanging on as it is." A tear trailed down his cheek. "I had to keep it together long enough to find you. You have to run. Go to Shadow City. The alpha, Atticus Bodle, will protect you, but trust only him with what you really are."

"Dad, how do we know it's not him attacking us?" My voice cracked. Atticus was the only person outside of the pack who knew of our existence, so it would make sense if this assault had to be on his orders.

"Atticus is a good man. I have never sensed any negative intent in him. I'm certain he isn't behind this, but be careful, and don't trust anyone else. One of the attackers said they're here to find you. We can't let them catch you."

"I... I don't want to leave you." Not only did he expect me to leave him behind, but he wanted me to go to a city I knew very little about.

"Baby girl, I love you, but you have to." He kissed my cheek. "They're gathering a small group to search for you. Go. Before it's too late."

"The alpha is missing," someone shouted from not too far away. "He may be searching for the girl."

I looked at my father one last time, trying to remember his smell, his face, his touch. "Daddy."

"I'm sorry, but I have to protect you." His eyes glowed a brighter silver as he called his last bit of strength. Alpha will laced his words. "Leave. Now. And don't come back."

My wolf howled in protest as I turned and my feet moved on their own accord, following our alpha's command. I glanced over my shoulder to look at him once more. "I love you, Daddy." I placed the knife back in the holster on my ankle and took off as I heard him drop.

"He's here," another guy yelled.

My wolf surged forward, helping me run as sobs racked me. I didn't want to leave, but I could not disobey my alpha.

The voices grew louder as multiple footsteps rushed toward my dad.

"I smell her!" someone exclaimed. "She's in the woods!"

Breathing deep again to calm myself down, I focused on putting one foot in front of the other. I had to get out of here before they caught me. My pack's sacrifice couldn't be in vain.

CHAPTER TWO

"**H**er scent is strong," one of the men yelled. "She can't be far."

Dammit, I didn't have even a quarter-mile lead on them. I had to get my head on straight or they'd capture me.

The urgency of my situation called for focus. At least, I had a reprieve from the overwhelming grief that wanted to suffocate me.

Wiping the moisture from my eyes and the snot from my nose, I increased my pace. They might have numbers on me, but I knew the land.

I veered left, staying deep enough in the woods that I couldn't be seen if they drove the roads. I ran a sporadic route, hoping they wouldn't guess that I was heading to the closest town, about four or five miles away. Luckily, the road led southwest toward Shadow City and allowed me to stay close to civilization. That would force the people chasing me to keep their animal sides at bay.

After all, humans weren't supposed to know about supernaturals. If someone let it slip, the punishment was death.

Footsteps pounded behind me, pushing me to move faster. I ran often for training, so I should be able to lose their asses. As long as I kept ahead, I should be okay.

I'd figure out what to do once I got closer to the city.

MY LEGS GREW HEAVY, and it took twice as much energy to keep going, but I pushed through the fatigue. From what I could guess, I'd run about fifteen miles, which meant Shadow City wasn't far ahead. If I maintained my current speed, I would reach the city in the next thirty minutes.

I was making decent time, but the assholes after me hadn't fallen behind as I'd hoped. I had to lose them.

Scanning the area, I searched for something that would slow them down. Staying close to the road wasn't a viable option any longer.

I cut to the right, farther away from the road, hoping the switch in direction would disorient them for a short while, and examined my surroundings. I wasn't familiar with this part of the woods. Even though our pack lived somewhat close to Shadow City, we'd always kept a wide berth from it, purposely avoiding anyone who lived near there.

I tried to remember everything I knew about Shadow City. It was a refuge that had been created over a thousand years ago. Anyone who needed help or asylum could go there. All shifter races lived there together, plus angels, vampires, witches... almost every supernatural race in existence.

When the city was founded, the silver wolves had been its protectors until corruption took hold. Unable to fight the corrupt leaders and unwilling to die for them, the silver wolves had chosen to leave.

At the time, Shadow City's alpha wolf had promised to clean the place up and had asked for us to not go too far away. Then, shortly after the silver wolves left, the city went into lockdown, not letting anyone in or out until the past few years.

Dad had gone there about two years ago, to meet with the current alpha wolf, Atticus, but he'd left me behind, telling me he needed to vet the situation and that I was to stay with the pack in case things went awry. I'd been sixteen then, old enough to step into the alpha role if necessary.

Despite the alpha's promise that things had gotten better, Dad had been wary of some of the other leaders in the city, specifically the angel, Azbogah, and some of the witches. Atticus had said to give him time, that we'd see more change. However, Dad never heard from him again.

For him to tell me to go there meant the Shadow City pack was my only hope for safety. That didn't sit well with me, but that was a problem for another day.

Right now, I had to get these assholes off my trail.

The rushing of the river helped me form an idea. I probably should've done it a while ago, but I'd foolishly thought I could outrun them.

Mistakes were forgivable as long as you could do something about them. And fortunately, I was alive and still moving, which meant everything in my current situation. No one else in my pack could say that.

"She's changing course," someone huffed. "She's heading for the river."

At least, they were showing signs of fatigue too. It would've sucked if they didn't sound as winded as I felt.

"Don't let her get there," another one yelled. "I'm calling for backup. We can't lose her."

The good thing about changing directions—it made

their weight shift on their feet. I hadn't been able to get a good read on how many were chasing me, but with them pivoting, it sounded like about ten were riding my ass.

That was more than I'd expected. I'd hoped for a handful. With that many, my odds of getting away were a whole lot slimmer.

A problem for after I reached the water.

Watching the ground closely, I looked for patches of mud, roots, and tree branches that could make me stumble or fall. Unfortunately, this slowed me down, but that was marginally safer than taking a tumble. Another reason I'd stayed close to the road—more stable ground.

The downward slope helped me run faster. Tree branches cut my arms, causing some bleeding, but nothing that fazed me. I barely felt the burn and the sting, but what was all too easy to feel was that I was their fucking prey. Something that angered both my wolf and me.

Their footsteps grew louder, alerting me that they were catching up. They were larger than me, so gravity worked in their favor.

I hadn't thought the plan through, but the river grew closer.

As long as I reached it before they caught up, I should be good. My plan was to go underwater and swim for as long as possible so they'd lose sight of me and my scent.

"I see her!" one of them shouted, way too close for comfort.

Ignoring the overwhelming urge to look over my shoulder, I pressed forward.

Murky water appeared between some trees as the Tennessee River came into view. The water didn't appear to move fast, but that was misleading. In spring, there was so much rain that the current was strong. Luckily, the section down here didn't have heavy traffic. The boats stayed mostly north of us, so it wasn't risky to swim around here.

My attackers' breathing was so loud that I could tell they were almost on top of me. If things didn't change drastically, they'd catch me before I reached the river.

I hadn't run over fifteen miles to be captured now.

Concentrating on my goal, I threw caution to the wind and hauled ass, no longer caring about my footing. I pumped my arms at my sides, trying to make my feet move even faster.

As I reached the embankment, the mulch turned into muddy stone, and I leaped.

"No," a guy screamed as something snagged my right ankle.

Twisting my body to the right, I used my left foot to kick the punk in the face. His head snapped back, and his grip on me loosened.

I fell on my back, barely short of the water, my head dangling off the edge of the embankment. I raised my head to see nine men stalking up only a few yards away from me.

If I didn't do something, they'd catch me before I hit the water.

The guy I'd kicked was knocked out, so I climbed over and grabbed his gun. I hated using guns, but right now, it was a necessity. I stood and fired at the rest of the men, who were too close for comfort.

"Take cover," one yelled as all nine scattered. I waited a second before firing again, keeping a random pattern in hopes that they'd wait to ensure I was done firing before racing after me again.

Not far away, the river curved sharply. If I could hold my breath long enough, I could still lose them. After a few more random gunshots, I squatted so they couldn't get a good visual. I fired once again then let my natural instincts take over. I flipped backward and hit the water feet first, sinking under the surface, and swam as hard as I could, using the current to my advantage.

I swam deeper, hoping the extra cloudiness of the water left over from the storms would hide me. A few bubbles hit my leg, informing me that at least some of them had jumped in but that I'd gained some distance.

Swimming was one of my favorite pastimes, something I was grateful for now as I kicked as hard as I could with the current to get as far ahead as possible. My lungs began to burn, needing oxygen. I exhaled a little, trying to prolong the time before I would inevitably need to resurface.

After several more strokes, I had to emerge. Trying to be careful, I allowed only the top of my face to break through the water, hoping to stay hidden.

"Look, there she is," one of them yelled.

Dammit. I submerged once more and let panic push me harder than before. I couldn't let them catch me. If I did, then all the lives sacrificed for me would be in vain.

I couldn't live with that.

With each stroke, I expected to be grabbed, but it didn't happen... at least, not yet.

I swam diagonally, hoping to catch a stronger current. When my lungs began to scream again, the water pushed against my back, propelling me forward.

Good, but I needed to replenish my air supply.

I waited as long as I could before my instincts took over and my arms pushed me toward the surface. However, the current wouldn't release me, and I was too weak to break through.

Panic seized my body, and my brain grew lightheaded. If I didn't get a hold of myself, I'd drown. Quickly, I flipped onto my back and stretched out my body, feet first. All the articles I'd read about river safety said to float with my head upstream and my legs down. Being horizontal to the water should help, at least marginally.

Surprisingly, getting into that position was easy once I wasn't *trying* to break through.

Something brushed my hand, and I grasped it. For all I knew, I could be holding hands with a corpse, but I was desperate enough to use whatever was available for leverage. Hopefully, it was a log. I yanked it toward me with the little bit of energy I had left. The edges of my vision started to darken, and I pushed the maybe-log down toward the riverbed, trying to use it to propel myself upward.

The momentum shifted me from the current, and when I broke through the top of the water, I sucked in a breath. My head was still foggy, and I spun around, looking for the assholes who'd put me in this situation, to begin with. A large tree branch floated beside me, so I threw my arms over it, no longer strong enough to stay afloat on my own.

My eyes grew heavy with exhaustion. Fighting for awareness, I craned my neck around but didn't see the douchebags.

I was safe for now, so I propped my head and body on the branch as best I could and closed my eyes to rest for a moment.

AN ARM WRAPPED around my waist, causing my heart to race and my breathing to quicken. I opened my eyes and realized that my dumb ass had fallen asleep. I had no clue for how long, but it was obviously long enough for them to catch up to me.

I kept hold of the branch and slammed my elbow into the prick's stomach. "Let go of me!"

"Whoa," a deep voice exclaimed and then groaned. "You're going to drown. I'm trying to save you." His hold around my waist slackened.

Did he think I'd actually fall for that? He didn't smell of a lie, but that didn't mean he had good intentions.

Since he was distracted by his stomach ailment, I head-butted him with the back of my head. A sickening crack informed me that I broke something.

"Fuck!" he complained as he pushed the log toward the embankment.

My legs made contact with the riverbed, and I put weight on them before falling back into the water with a large splash.

"Hey, wait," the guy said as he swam over to me.

"Stay back." With trembling hands, I pulled my knife from the sheath and held it in front of me as I glared. "I will hurt you."

"Obviously." He gestured to the blood pouring from his nose. "You already have." Drops of water fell from his short, dark hair and dripped onto a once sky-blue shirt and jeans. The warmth of dark chocolate eyes caused me to lose focus, and my hand dropped a couple of inches. He had the musky scent of a shifter, but he was in human form.

He wasn't wearing black, but he could still be one of them, messing with me. I had no clue how long I'd been out, and he could've changed into a different outfit and jumped in after me.

I lifted my chin and raised the knife. "Who are you?" I had no clue how I was going to get out of here. I didn't have the strength to stand, for God's sake.

"I'm Killian." He moved his hand slowly to his nose and

pinched the bridge. "Killian Green. I saw you floating on a tree limb and thought you might be in trouble."

"Why would you think that?" I kept my body facing forward as I scanned for other possible attackers. They were probably hiding in the woods, waiting for the sign.

"Did you not hear what I said?" The corners of his mouth tipped upward. "You were passed out, floating on a tree limb in the middle of the river. It's dangerous to be swimming right now after the heavy storms that passed through."

"And you happened to be out here?" I had a hard time buying it.

He pointed toward a tree at the edge of the water. "Fishing."

Against my better judgment, my gaze followed where he motioned. And sure enough, a rod was propped against a tree with a worm dangling on the hook. The poor worm wiggled like it might have a chance to survive.

"So you aren't trying to capture me?" The words tumbled from my lips before I could stop them.

His brows furrowed, and he released his hold on his nose and wiped off the blood. "No, but now I understand why you beat the shit out of me." He chuckled.

"You find that humorous?" He had to be some sort of sick asshole to find the fact that I was almost kidnapped amusing.

He grimaced. "No, I'm sorry. It's just, there's only one girl who has ever kicked my ass like you did." He tilted his head as he examined me. "And funnily enough, you remind me of her." He frowned like he was remembering someone he didn't want to.

This was getting uncomfortable, and for me, staying close to the water wasn't smart. They'd be combing the area, looking for me. "Look, I've got to go. It's not safe here for me." I placed both hands in front of me to bear some of my weight as I stood. Slowly, I climbed to my feet even though my legs wanted to buckle again. I took one step and dropped.

Before I could make impact, a strong arm caught me around the waist.

"Let me help you." He glanced around the area. "You're not going to make it far in this condition."

I hated that he was right. "Fine." I kept a strong hold on my knife, ready to use it at any given moment.

We slowly made it out of the water and to the tree line. But I wouldn't feel better until I was hidden. After a few steps on land, I stumbled into the woods.

"Hey, where do you think you're going?" Killian asked. "You can't leave like that."

And there it was. He hadn't been helping me after all.

CHAPTER THREE

I spun on my heel and tried not to fall over. Almost drowning had taken a hell of a lot out of me, but I had to push through and get to safety before I could fall apart.

My arm shook as I lifted the knife in his direction again. "So, you are working with them?"

"With who?" His forehead creased, and he lifted a hand. "You can barely walk."

"Don't worry." I took a slow step in his direction and almost pumped my fist in celebration when my knees didn't buckle. Who cared if it took every ounce of concentration to pull it off? Confidence spoke wonders. "I can still kick your ass."

"In fairness, I didn't fight against you," he said and rubbed his nose, emphasizing the crooked section that I'd broken. "You can barely stand, and even though you caught me off guard, I didn't hurt you."

"Stop rambling, and let's get this over with." I didn't want to hear about how pathetic I was. If he was going to force me to leave with him, we could bypass the chitchat.

"Look—" He walked slowly toward me like I was some sort of cornered animal.

Adrenaline coursed through me, making my body a little more sturdy. I swung my arm, trying to slice his chest.

He growled as he jumped back, the sharp edge narrowly missing him. "You need to calm down."

The momentum of missing him threw my body off balance, and I caught myself before I could fall. "Not happening." I stood back on my feet, ready to attack again.

"I'm trying to tell you—" he started, but I jumped toward him.

He spun away from my attack, and I landed hard on my feet, jarring my neck.

Before I could face him again, a hand gripped the wrist that held the knife, and an arm snaked around my neck. He pushed his weight on me so I had to kneel.

Here it was. What I'd been waiting for. My breathing grew rapid as I strained to hear some sign of the others.

"Calm down," Killian commanded. "I'm not going to hurt you."

"Really?" I spat. "Because this doesn't feel great." I'd never felt so weak before. I hated the feeling and never wanted to experience it again.

"You obviously have someone hunting you, and you almost drowned." He blew out a breath. "I was trying to be understanding, but you forced my hand."

"Where are the others?" I lifted my head, scanning the woods.

"There are no others," he said exasperatedly. "I keep trying to tell you this. You are safe. No one is here to get you."

I waited for the sulfuric scent of a lie to hit me, but

nothing came. "So you came out here alone in human form to fish?"

"Yes." He sighed. "It was my sister's favorite spot."

Was.

She must be dead.

Dad's face flickered in my head. *Mom. Zoe.* Grief tried to wash over me, but I couldn't let it. At least, not yet. I wasn't safe. "I'm sorry about breaking your nose, but I need to leave."

"I gathered that," he said, but his hold didn't slacken.

"They'll be combing the river, and it won't take long before they get here." Actually, I had no clue where I was. "If you release me, I'll go without causing you any more issues."

His arm loosened slightly. "Are we good now?"

"Yeah." I dropped the knife, letting him know I had no intention of using it.

"Thank God." He let go of me and stood. "Who the hell is chasing you?"

That was a question I had myself. "No clue."

I picked up my knife, making him tense.

"I thought you said we were good." His eyes glowed faintly, his wolf peeking through.

I locked eyes with him as I bent down and placed the knife back in my sheath. "We are, but I'm not going to leave this behind." I placed a hand on a tree trunk, letting it brace my weight as I stood. When I felt steady enough on my feet, I strolled farther into the woods.

The sooner I moved out of the area, the faster my scent would dissipate, which would make finding me harder.

"Hey, wait up," Killian called as I heard him run back to the river.

There was no way I was waiting. Considering how slow I was moving, he'd be able to catch up to me in no time.

No matter how much I pushed myself, my speed never increased. I bet a freaking turtle could have beaten me.

"Of course she didn't wait for me," he grumbled. "She's too damn headstrong, like Olive." He trudged in my direction.

In a matter of seconds, he caught up to me, his fishing pole slung over his shoulder. He bit his bottom lip. "So, where are you heading?"

"I shouldn't tell you." If somehow they figured out he'd run into me, they'd torture him for information. "The less you know, the safer you'll be."

"Okay, so, if you don't know who, do you know *why* they're after you?" He slowed his pace to walk beside me.

"Once again, best if you don't know." What was with all the questions? "So, where exactly am I?"

"You don't know?" He pursed his lips. "How long were you out?"

I couldn't keep the venom out of my words. "If I knew that, I wouldn't be asking where I was now, would I?" I grimaced, immediately regretting biting his head off. I blew a raspberry. "Look, I'm sorry."

A smile flitted on his face. "For what exactly? Punching me in the gut, breaking my nose, trying to stab me, or being rude?"

Ouch. "In fairness, I thought you were an attacker. So, in this instance, I'm purely talking about biting your head off."

He chuckled. "Fair enough."

"Is withholding information my punishment?" I felt comfortable around him, which was odd. Normally, when I was around other wolf shifters, I got nervous and anxious, afraid I'd slip up and give them a hint of what I was.

"Maybe." He waggled his eyebrows. "But in all seriousness, you've landed in Shadow Ridge."

My shoulders sagged with relief. No way. Could I actually have gotten this lucky? Granted, after a day like today, I deserved some kind of break. "The bordering wolf shifter town to Shadow City?"

"The very one." He tilted his head. "You seem relieved."

"I am." I guessed there was no point in not telling him now. Maybe he could help me. "I was instructed to come to Shadow City, so all I need to do is get there."

"You do realize you can't go into the city without permission, right?" He wrung the hem of his shirt as if getting the excess water out would improve his situation.

"Atticus Bodle will see me." That had to be why Dad had mentioned the alpha's name. He'd be my ticket inside.

"Uh." He scratched the back of his neck. "Atticus won't be able to help you."

My stomach dropped. "Why?" Something bad must have happened. That must have been why Dad hadn't heard from him the past couple of years. "Is he in trouble?"

"That's one way of putting it." Killian cleared his throat. "He died almost two years ago."

This day kept getting worse and worse. "No." That was my entire plan. I'd banked everything on getting into the city and seeing Atticus. I hadn't even considered the possibility that Dad's instructions would have a flaw. He always knew what to do, but as of today, that officially had changed. The worst part was I didn't have him here to counsel me. "That's not possible."

"I assure you it is." He nibbled on his bottom lip.

"Shadow City residents that attended his funeral saw his dead body. It was open casket."

"You didn't attend?" My stomach tightened even more.

"No." He shook his head. "I'm not allowed inside yet. They're slowly opening the city."

"How did he die?" I asked, even though the answer wouldn't help my situation.

He huffed. "Heart attack."

I must have misheard him. There was no way. "Wasn't he young?" Shifters lived to be well over a hundred, and Dad had made it sound like Atticus was only a couple of years his senior. A heart attack was very unusual.

"That's what made it so shocking." Killian took a few steps. "But being the alpha in Shadow City is a tough job. From what I've been told, navigating pack politics and trying to represent all the shifter races fairly while working with the council members is more stressful than anyone can imagine. The extreme stress made his heart give out."

I stopped in my tracks as my stomach dropped. I had nowhere to go. No plan to execute.

Nothing.

My heart pounded. My head spun, and my throat closed.

"Hey!" Killian said. "What's wrong?"

Not able to respond, I tried to focus on filling my lungs, but it was like my body had frozen.

"Girl." He grumbled to himself, "I don't even know her name."

I bent my knees, not able to stand upright any longer. I had to get control of this panic attack or I'd pass out again, but I didn't know how to. I'd never felt this pathetic before.

"This is going to hurt me more than it'll hurt you," he said.

A hard slap hit the side of my face. The sting broke through the suffocating haze. I sucked in a breath, filling my lungs.

"Are you okay?" He leaned over me as he examined my face.

"No, I'm not." The severity of the truth blasted like a bomb. I shouldn't have admitted it, but he would've known if I had lied. "Atticus was my only hope. I don't have any money or even clothing to my name. I don't know what to do." Here I was, pouring my heart out to a stranger, but it somehow felt right.

"Well, then I guess it's a damn good thing I found you." He brushed my cheek where he'd slapped me. His fingers were rough and warm.

I'd never been touched like that by anyone except my parents, but the different sensations I'd expected to feel didn't come. "What do you mean?"

"My best friend might be able to help you." He winked at me. "And I have a huge house all to myself."

"You own a house?" I asked with disbelief. He couldn't be that much older than me, but that didn't mean anything. Since I'd lived in such a small, close-knit community where generations of families lived together in the same house, anyone getting their own house was a big deal. Living situations were probably quite different outside of our hidden little world.

His face creased. "I inherited it when my family died three years ago."

Tears burned my eyes. "I'm so sorry. I lost my family too." And if I didn't start moving, I'd break down. The poor guy had already seen me ridden with anxiety and weak from almost drowning. I didn't need to add emotionally broken to that. Maybe I could push my breakdown out another hour.

He easily kept pace with me as the backside of a neighborhood came into sight through the trees. The houses appeared to be craftsman style, and one of them had a large pool in the backyard.

He frowned. "How long ago?"

"Earlier today." My voice ached with sadness. "The men chasing me—they killed everyone. My dad told me to run and find Atticus. That's why I came all the way here and why I thought you wanted to catch me."

"Well, that settles it." He smiled, but it didn't reach his eyes. "You'll be staying with me."

"I couldn't." I didn't want to be a burden. "That's asking way too much."

"First off, you didn't ask." He held up one finger then added a second. "And second, you have nowhere to go. You're not in the best of health since you almost drowned, and you have no money to your name. Not to mention, people are hunting you." He touched my arm. "And honestly, it gets lonely in the house, but I can't seem to get myself to move. You'd be keeping me company."

The word *yes* was on the tip of my tongue, but I didn't want to take advantage of him. "Are you sure?"

"Yeah." He waved a hand in front of me. "Besides, you're soaking wet. You won't be able to go anywhere without raising some eyebrows."

He was right. I wouldn't be able to go anywhere unnoticed, not that I had money anyway. "Okay, but I don't want anyone to know about me or what happened to my family." If word of that got out, it could help whoever was hunting me locate me.

"Got it. You can trust me." He led me to the yard that

had the large in-ground pool with a diving board and water slide. "This is our stop."

"You live close." His fishing spot on the riverbank was only about a mile from his home.

He walked past the pool and up some brick stairs leading to a covered back porch. Thankfully, the porch's floor was cement, so I wouldn't ruin anything by dripping all over it.

"Let me grab you a towel, and I'm pretty sure my sister's clothes will fit you." He opened the door, which had been left unlocked.

"Your sister?" I cringed, thinking about wearing his dead sister's clothes. "Are you sure?"

"Yeah. I mean, they should do someone some good." His shoulders sagged, and he smiled sadly. "I'll be right back." He slipped inside, leaving me alone.

A chill ran down my spine, and I turned to face the woods. I rubbed my arms and assessed my surroundings. I needed to get a feel for the area and devise an escape plan in case they found me here. I couldn't stay and put innocent lives at risk.

The house next door appeared to have the same layout as this one, but instead of the hunter-green color of Killian's, it was pure white. A large fire pit had been dug out back with beer cans scattered around. Whoever lived there must be a drinker, or maybe they had people over routinely. That could be a good thing though—it would mix my smell with several others and help to obscure it.

Killian's footsteps grew closer to the door, and I turned as it opened.

He had changed into a white shirt and jeans. After handing me a large beach towel, he gestured through a pris-tine kitchen, past the wide-open living room with a picture of him and his family hanging above the couch, toward a hallway on the other end of the house. "If you go to the second room on the left, that's Olive's room. You can go through her closet and pick out something to change into. When you're done, come on out, and we'll get something to eat."

"Thank you." Even if I wanted to argue, I couldn't. He was being generous and helping me. I toweled off as best I could and hurried to the bedroom.

Inside, I shut the door and laid my head against it. I expected the grief to hit again, but numbness filled me instead.

Good. First step, get dry. I pulled off my clothes and walked toward the white queen-size canopy bed with a plum comforter, noting the matching white end tables and dresser. The walls were lavender, almost the shade of the purple of my eyes. The shaggy cream carpet felt amazing under my feet as I padded to the closet beside the bed.

As I surveyed the room, a picture on the end table caught my attention. It was of a younger Killian and a girl who must be his sister at the embankment, fishing together. They could almost pass for twins. Killian had his arm slung over her shoulders.

The fact that he'd lost his own family and now had found me had to be fate. We could both understand the pain of loss.

Choosing not to wear her underwear, I slipped on a thick black shirt and gray sweatpants. My stomach gurgled, and I grabbed my wet clothes and the towel then headed back to the kitchen.

Killian was nowhere to be seen, so I placed my clothes on the glass circular kitchen table and used the towel to dry the water I'd dripped on the hardwood floors. I'd squatted to finish wiping the floor when I heard him outside on the back porch.

"Hey, man," he whispered. "Yeah, I'm not going to make it tonight. Something came up."

Great, I was already interfering with his social life. I would have felt bad, but he had insisted on me staying.

After a moment, he spoke again. "Yeah, there's this girl I want to tell you about."

No. He'd promised he wouldn't tell a soul.

CHAPTER FOUR

I t was time to get the hell out of here. If he was already telling people about me, those men would find me easily. Leaving the towel on the floor, I gathered my wet clothes and moved toward the front door, my feet pounding on the hardwood. Then I came to an abrupt stop.

Dammit. I wasn't wearing shoes.

Should I leave without grabbing my soaked tennis shoes or take the extra time and grab them?

The longer I spent contemplating my options, the more likely he'd catch me before I escaped. A quick decision needed to be made.

Being barefoot would garner more attention, so taking the time to get them was the best option.

Making a mad dash back to Killian's sister's room, I tried to focus on one task at a time. Dad always said, *If you get too many steps ahead, you make mistakes on the most pressing ones.* I could almost hear his voice.

Almost.

And my heart somehow fractured a little more.

Focus, Sterlyn, I chastised myself as I slipped the shoes on. Water gushed around my toes, making me pause.

The back door opened, and Killian stepped inside.

There went my plan of sneaking out. Nonetheless, that didn't change my need to leave. I'd already been leery of staying here, and knowing I couldn't trust him made the decision to go so much easier. I hated that my instincts had been wrong, but I'd deal with that later.

Evolve and learn from your mistakes.

His footsteps echoed toward the room. "You're not changed yet?" Killian chuckled. "I figured you'd be out here, pacing the floor."

Dread pooled in my stomach. I'd had way too many confrontations today, but I might as well add another one. Putting it off would only make things worse.

I held the clothes harder against me, and more liquid absorbed into the dark shirt I'd put on. Apparently, there hadn't been a point in me changing after all.

"Uh..." He paused. "Dove?"

Dove? Maybe he hadn't been talking to me all along. Was someone else here? I sniffed, but all I smelled was him.

He knocked. "Are Olive's clothes not working?"

"Yeah, they're fine." I pushed my cowardice away and opened the door.

His eyebrows shot upward, and he smirked. "The point of changing was to get dry." He gestured to the wet clothes against my chest.

"And the point of asking you to not tell someone about me was for you *not* to call someone at the first opportunity and spill my secrets." My voice rose as my anger bled through. I shoved past him, marching toward the front door.

"Hey, wait," he said as he followed me and gently grabbed my arm. "It's not what you think."

"Oh, so the whole 'there's a girl I want to tell you about' wasn't actually about me?" I lifted my chin, daring him to deny it.

"Give me a chance to explain." He raised a hand and gave me puppy dog eyes.

And the more insane part was that it worked. My resolve crumbled. "You've got one minute."

"You know how you were talking about how you didn't feel right staying here?" He jumped right to the point.

"Yes." This had to be some sort of trap, and I was walking right into it.

His dark eyes turned milk chocolate. "What if you staying here helps me too?"

"How so?" I hated to admit that I was intrigued.

He rubbed his hands together. "Date me."

I jerked back. "What?" I had to have heard him wrong.

"Date." He touched his chest. "Me."

"You seem great." He had lost his mind. Maybe when I'd punched him, I'd caused a brain injury. "But my family and entire pack were slaughtered this morning, and I'm kind of running for my life. Dating isn't high on the priority list." I edged toward the door. I didn't want to startle him. I'd heard fast movements could aggravate insanity.

"There won't be strings attached, only exclusivity." He motioned between us. "You need a place to live, and I need the pressure to date someone to go away. It's a win-win."

"You don't want to date someone, but you asked me to date you?" My head spun, and I was pretty sure it wasn't from almost drowning.

"I can understand why you'd be inching toward the door." He shook his head. "But it isn't as insane as it sounds. Like I said, we would date and be exclusive, but we'll be friends dating without the romantic pressure. There's this girl eyeing my best friend, and she's pushing her best friend at me. I'm not interested, but I can't get Luna to leave me alone."

Wow, so much information at one time, but I had nowhere else to go. "So, you want to date me for real, but we're just friends. Nothing would be actually expected from me... in any capacity—physically or otherwise."

"Exactly." He blew out a breath. "I mean, you're gorgeous, and you're strong and direct, which reminds me of Olive. My sister. It's kind of nice being around you. It doesn't seem quite like she's gone."

Some of the discomfort fell from my chest, and surprisingly, his words didn't hurt my feelings. He was handsome, but I wasn't into him *that* way either. "If I agree, what does that have to do with the conversation with whomever it was earlier?" If he thought his weird proposal would distract me from that... it wouldn't.

"Well, this is where it gets awkward." He tugged at an ear. "I did tell Griffin—that's my best friend—about you, in the sense that I said I couldn't go out with that girl tonight because I was with you."

"You assumed I'd say yes?" My emotions were bouncing all over the place; I couldn't settle on one. I was equally horrified, angered, and flattered. It was a trifecta of conflict.

"Actually, it kind of came out, and I'm hoping you'll say yes, or I'm kinda screwed." He gestured to the house. "But this place is big enough for both of us. You can stay in Olive's room. Make it your own, and I'll stay in mine."

"This is a little crazy." And the funny thing was that I was downplaying it by calling it crazy. "I have nothing to my name—"

"Which makes this even more of a good plan." He took my clothes out of my hand. "I'm the alpha of Shadow Ridge, and I've got connections. I can help you get a fake ID and get you a job at the Shadow Ridge University coffee shop. You would have a secret identity with money and a place to live."

He was so young to have such a leadership role, but sometimes fate forced our hand. His help sounded a little too good to be true. "If you're alpha, that means others will be around a lot. I'm trying to blend in." Unless...maybe his pack being around would help with that. "Besides, why don't you tell that girl that you aren't interested? It would be a hell of a lot easier than doing all this other stuff."

"Don't worry about the pack. Honestly, I kind of stay out of their way. Even though I'm technically the alpha, I'm taking a hiatus, and my dad's beta is filling in. They're giving me space to go to college and grieve for my family, so you'll be more off the radar here than anywhere else." Sadness crept into his voice. "In regards to the girl, I've tried." He blew out a breath. "The problem isn't even her—it's her best friend, who keeps pushing for us to go out. The best friend is close with Griffin because her dad works with him. Griffin doesn't see that she's trying to force his hand to settle down. So, me having a girlfriend will make things easier with a lot less drama than continually refusing them."

He had no clue how girls worked. This would cause even more drama. Girls like that didn't back down without a fight. But a fake ID would be an amazing thing to have, and maybe his messed-up life could distract me from mine. "And I'd get to keep the fake ID?" With that, I could get a plane ticket or whatever else I might need when verifying my identity would be involved.

"Yup," he said and beamed as if he knew he had me. "I know we're being secretive, so I haven't even bothered asking your name. But is there a name you want on the ID?"

"Uh..." I chewed on my lip. I had so much on my mind; I didn't have the capacity to add anything else to it. "Surprise me?" I squeaked.

"Can do." He scratched his neck. "Any other information I should know?"

"Nope." I got that he was curious, but I'd told him enough for one day. "I'm facted out for now."

"Then let me make it official." He got down on one knee and lifted a hand. "Will you please do the honor of being my girlfriend?"

Somehow, he didn't look completely ridiculous. "Yes, I will, but why me? You're attractive. I'm sure you could find someone to date without bribing me."

"I'll be real. Like I said, I lost my entire family too. I know what it feels like, and maybe by helping you, I'll find some peace. Because I still can't look in the mirror." His eyes glistened, and he turned toward the living room and sniffled.

Absolution was what he was after. If I hadn't been leaning toward saying yes by this point, that would've changed my mind.

He pretended to scratch his nose when he was wiping under his eye before facing me again. "Our group is pretty steady. Not a lot of new faces, so me having a girlfriend will be more believable with a newbie in town. Especially since I sort of slept with most everyone here already."

Of course he had. "Wow. It's a good thing that sex is off the table." I wanted to make him smile again. "No telling what kind of STDs I could've gotten otherwise."

"Ha. Ha." He glowered. "We can't catch STDs."

"So...you've tried?" I bantered back, feeling oddly at ease.

"I believe in trying anything fun." He winked as he

headed back toward the kitchen. "Now, go change again. I need to take a picture of you to send to my buddy for your new ID, and then I'll start some hamburgers. We need to get you fed."

AN ALARM BLARED, startling me from sleep. My eyelids were so heavy I almost had to pry them open with my fingers. I'd slept hard, but not well, the entire night.

Dreams had haunted me.

I'd lost count of the number of times I'd killed the guy behind my house. Each time, the pain felt fresh. Being a protector, I'd grown up knowing that the chance of killing someone was always there. But doing it was different than what I'd expected.

When I wasn't dreaming of killing, the images of my slaughtered pack were there.

So much blood.

So much hate.

Everyone I loved was gone. Almost like they'd never existed.

And the scariest part was someone was hunting me, and the only clue I had as to why was when Goatee had mentioned breeding with me. The thought of being forced to birth more silver wolves petrified me.

The memory of my dad bleeding out while commanding me to leave ended each cycle. Every time, that was the final blow. The last straw that had me falling apart.

Without them, I didn't know who I was anymore.

A rogue wolf with no one to turn to. Where my pack links had been was now cold. Completely cold. No-survivors cold. If I didn't connect again soon, insanity would start creeping in, and from what I'd heard, it might be only weeks before the madness took over. I had to find a pack fast...but that would mean letting someone in on my secret.

That wasn't possible. At least, not now.

The realization was the final piercing of my already unstable heart.

I didn't have time for this. Life moved on. The world still turned. And my heart still beat even if it felt like it shouldn't.

Somehow finding the strength within, I reached over and turned off the alarm. Even though my eyes stayed heavy, I forced myself out of the comfortable bed. I wasn't ready to face those dreams again.

I made the bed, trying to keep the negative thoughts at bay. Doing a routine task was comforting. I smoothed the bedspread into place before turning to the closet, trying to determine what to wear for an interview at a coffee shop.

Surprisingly, last night wasn't horrible. Killian had known what to do to help me process things. He hadn't asked about my family or pack but instead told me stories about his own, including their tragic deaths.

With tear-filled eyes, he recapped the entire nightmare. He was supposed to go with his parents, sister, and a few other shifters to a nearby lake to look into some strange occurrences that had happened there, but it was the same timing as some sort of senior high school party. He'd bailed on them last minute to attend the party instead, and everyone who'd gone had been jumped and killed. As soon as their pack heard through their links that they were in danger, people had rushed to help them. But they'd been far away enough that no one reached them in time.

There had been no survivors.

Similar to my own story.

He blamed himself. If he'd gone with them, maybe things would've been different. Because of that failure, he wasn't mentally ready to lead the Shadow Ridge pack like his father, Orion. He only attended meetings and made decisions when absolutely necessary, and he trusted his beta, Billy, to take care of the day-to-day pack matters. He kept himself somewhat isolated from the pack because he felt like he'd failed them already.

Part of me wanted to comfort him, but how could I when I felt the same way? If anything, I understood exactly where he was coming from.

When I'd stayed quiet, he'd popped popcorn and turned on a comedy featuring pure relationship angst. No killing, no family triggers, nothing but a girl and a boy finding their way to each other.

Pursing my lips, I flipped through the closet. His sister had drastically different tastes than me. There were several dresses, skirts, and flowy tops instead of the jeans and shirts that I always wore. All the other items were old worn shirts that looked like she'd used them for bumming around the house.

A college coffee shop should be pretty casual, but I didn't want to wear baggy clothes. Ugh. I was going to have to suck it up and wear something that I didn't want to. The best option I could find was a ruffled apricot dress. The sleeves were three-quarter length, which fit the spring season, and the hem stopped several inches above my knees. I paired the dress with some black flats that were a smidge too big for my feet.

When I received my first paycheck, I'd go clothes shopping.

Trying not to dwell on my misfortune, I glanced in the mirror. The fact that it didn't shatter astounded me. My hair was one huge rat's nest. I had bloodshot eyes and dark circles underneath.

The hair was my own fault. I'd taken a shower and fallen into bed without drying it. Now I had to get to work on myself to come off somewhat presentable.

A FEW MINUTES LATER, Killian knocked on my door. "Dove?"

That was the second time he'd called me that. What the hell?

I took one last look in the mirror, relieved that I looked nearly normal after working the knots from my hair. Inhaling sharply, I opened the door and found Killian leaning against the wall in front of me.

"Why do you keep calling me Dove?"

"You never told me your name, so I improvised." He gestured to my hair. "And your hair is gray, reminding me of dove feathers. I bet it's hard to keep that color up."

My name was on the tip of my tongue, but I didn't let it fall. And the fact that he thought my hair was dyed made things easier on my end. I'd never had a nickname before, and it was safer for both of us if he didn't know my real one. "That works."

"You like it?" He smiled. "It's unique, like you. You've already become Dove in my head, so even if you told me your real name, you'd be stuck with it."

In my pack, everyone had treated me as their leader, even though I hadn't yet taken the position. The only one who'd treated me like a regular person had been Zoe, but she never went so far as to give me a pet name.

The image of my lifeless best friend filled my mind—her

gorgeous espresso hair disheveled and blood pooling from her mouth. What I'd do to be able to save her. To hear her give me shit once again.

"Hey," Killian rasped. "Are you with me?"

"Uh... yeah." That was such a strange question. "I'm right in front of you."

"I meant mentally." He booped my nose. "You seemed far away."

That wasn't good. I needed to at least give the illusion I was present. By not being alert, I was already failing at being a good protector. "Yeah, ready to go."

"Then your chariot awaits." He flipped his hands in the direction of the kitchen. "The garage is through here."

In the garage, I found a black truck that looked brand new. Within seconds, we were in the truck, pulling out and heading toward Shadow Ridge University.

Killian glanced in my direction, and I realized my leg was bouncing fitfully against the black leather. I forced it to stop and examined the truck's interior. This was a newer model that had all the bells and whistles. On a cold day, the seat warmer would feel like heaven.

As we drove through the quaint downtown, I scanned the buildings. The road was two lanes lined with parking meters outside of brick shops that connected for a couple of miles. There were restaurants, banks, and a movie theater. Everything that you'd expect to find in a town.

As we stopped at a red light, the door to a breakfast restaurant opened, and a guy wearing all black with an auburn goatee stepped out.

My heart froze as he locked eyes with me.

CHAPTER FIVE

The car closed in around me, and my lungs stopped
working. The morning took on a surreal quality. If
the attackers had found my trail, I'd expect them to track me
straight to Killian's home, not go eat breakfast at a diner in
the middle of town.

What was their end game? Maybe they needed to refuel
before coming after me again.

My strength was returning now that the new moon was
over, but that wasn't comforting at all. They should have
struck hard and fast while I remained weak.

Killian spoke, but I couldn't make sense of his words.
My attention was focused entirely on the man I was sure
was Goatee. Our gazes were still locked, and the hair on the
back of my neck stood on end. Could we have it out in the
middle of the town square?

My hands clenched as the door to the diner opened and
three men joined Goatee on the curb.

"We need to go," I said through gritted teeth as Goatee
looked away and focused on his friends.

This would be where he warned them, and they'd

attack. I hadn't brought my knife because of this stupid-ass dress, and now I regretted it. I had no weapon against these assholes, which proved my training correct. We learned to always have something on hand.

"Go!" I shouted. We were still sitting at the red light like bumps on a log.

"I can't." Killian gestured to people walking through the crosswalk in front of us. "Or I'm going to hurt someone."

Of course we'd be stuck at a red light. It was like the universe was pushing me toward these assholes, and I didn't know why. I'd lost everything. Wasn't that enough?

All I could do was sit here and wait.

Wait for the gestures and shouts.

Wait for them to drag me from the car.

Wait for them to finish the job and hopefully kill me too.

I'd rather die than be forced into a relationship with the sole purpose of producing offspring. Could I even love children that came from a forced union? I was afraid the answer would be yes, which would mean that watching them grow up into horrible people would be the final torture my would-be kidnappers could bestow upon me.

"Dove?" Killian leaned over to look at the four guys, who turned and casually walked away.

My breathing hitched. They were walking away. I shook my head and sucked in the breath I so desperately needed.

The fog began to clear as I blinked. If they were my attackers, they wouldn't have walked away like that. The people chasing me had been bound and determined to get me. They would've struck immediately.

I was being paranoid. Surely there was more than one redhead in the world who wore a goatee.

As my body sagged, the truck pulled forward.

Killian touched my arm softly, but his voice contained an edge. "Did those guys do something to you?"

"No." If he hadn't thought I'd lost my marbles by now, he would after this. "But the one that walked out first reminded me of one of the attackers. I thought—" My voice failed me, and I sat there with my mouth hanging open.

"Hey, you're going to see their faces and probably your packs' faces sporadically." Pain laced his words. "Believe me. It's part of the denial process, or maybe the trauma of it all. And I wasn't the one who found my family dead. You're going to have it so much worse than me."

"So that was normal?" I grimaced. I didn't want that to be normal for me—a trauma survivor. But no one would ever choose this road.

Dad used to say our trials made us stronger. I always believed him... until now. How did my pack being decimated make any of us stronger?

They were dead.

There was no reason for what happened other than brutality. Something that made my blood boil more than the moonlight ever had.

"Yeah, it's normal." He placed both hands back on the steering wheel. "It fucking sucks. It's one reason that Griffin tries not to go back to Shadow City. There are so many memories of his dad there and all the plans they made together for the packs."

"Griffin?" Wait... That was who he was talking with last night. "Your best friend."

"The very one." Killian chuckled. "His dad died shortly after my parents, leaving him with a whole lot of responsibility, like me. Despite us meeting only a few years ago when Shadow City opened back up, our losses bonded us together quickly."

"Then why do you feel responsible for helping me?"

"I don't feel responsible." He tilted his head toward me. "I want to help you. There's a huge difference. Besides." He leaned back in his seat and placed a wrist over the steering wheel. "You're helping me in return, so it's mutually beneficial." He waggled his eyebrows.

And I laughed. So odd. Ten seconds ago, I was on the brink of a breakdown, and now he had me smiling. Maybe I was certifiable. "No waggling eyebrows at me. This is completely platonic dating that so happens to be exclusive."

He huffed and rolled his eyes. "You're no fun."

"No, I'm not." And just like that, the sadness took hold of my chest again. "I've lost too much to be fun." Add in the fact that Dad had been grooming me since birth to be the perfect alpha. He'd repeat that, if I was a boy, it would be so much easier. Times were changing, with more women leading packs, but, not fast enough. For me to not get challenged, I had to be even stronger and more poised.

Because of that, no one had ever approached me for a date. Everyone my age had thought I was too perfect, or they were intimidated. Zoe had been my one and only true friend, able to see past most of the act. Though not all.

"Hey, it'll be okay." His hand tightened on the steering wheel, making his knuckles turn white. "It has to be."

Silence descended between us, leaving both of us lost in our own thoughts. Ones that I didn't want to have but didn't have the strength to push away. Arian and Cassie Knight had been amazing parents, even when they were hard on me. Mom had a way of making things better whenever I grew too overwhelmed with expectations or training. And Dad made me feel stronger and taught me to believe in myself. Because of them, I hadn't been captured and had found the strength to get away even when the enemy got too close to catching me.

As we turned toward the woods and the flowing river, several large brick buildings about a mile away popped into view. They looked brand new.

"That's the university." Killian answered my unspoken question.

It was picturesque with enough acreage that my wolf could happily run for miles. The lawn in front almost looked artificial with healthy green grass. "This place is gorgeous."

He smiled. "It really is. All the buildings were constructed at one time so the campus has a cohesive feel and branding."

"Do humans go here too?" From the little bit I'd heard about it, I'd assumed Shadow City was populated only by supernaturals, but I wasn't sure about the surrounding towns.

"No." He shook his head. "It's all supernatural based, but to maintain appearances, we allow humans to apply. We have a thorough screening process to weed them out from actually being accepted. We want this to be a college where supernaturals get the kind of education they need for their future, whether that's leading, fighting, healing, and so forth."

"So there aren't any humans in Shadow Ridge either?" Being around only supernaturals unsettled me. All of my experiences visiting the small town near my pack's home had involved a human presence, and any other supernaturals who might live or visit the town always had to be careful to not ask certain questions. Here, it would be harder to keep my heritage hidden. I couldn't risk running in animal form because, if anyone had even a vague memory of silver wolves, they would peg me easily. Staying human was going to suck because I was used to shifting daily. It was part of our training regimen, to fight in both wolf and human form. But I'd manage.

I had to.

"No humans live here, but tourists come into town." He pursed his lips. "It's good for businesses since they spend a lot of money, and having them around helps us remember our human side."

His wording seemed odd, but I let it go. The buildings were growing closer, and I could see now that a wrought iron gate circled the campus.

As we approached the wrought iron fence that served as the main entrance, I could see the emblem of a city etched into it with the words Shadow Ridge University underneath.

"Is that a drawing of Shadow City?" The emblem had modern buildings with a paw print and a symbol attached to the top.

"Sure is."

"So you've been there?" If he had a way into the city, maybe I could figure out another person to contact. I could find out who'd replaced Atticus.

"Oh, no. There's a large wall and dome that keeps the city from view. In order to get in, you need permission from one of the council members. They're letting residents out freely now, but it's still hard to get inside if you don't already live there." He slowed the truck as we approached a guard shack sitting between the entrance and exit lanes. "But I've been told that's the skyline of the city."

The gates to the university were closed, and Killian rolled down his window as he stopped.

The guard took a step toward us even as Killian pulled out a card key and swiped it against the reader. The gate clicked and slowly opened.

"Doesn't traffic get backed up if everyone has to stop and scan in?" I glanced over my shoulder to find no one behind us.

What time did classes start? It was almost nine in the morning. I'd figured this place would be a lot busier.

"Half the students stay in the dorms here." He accelerated and rolled up his window. "The other two hundred or so, like yours truly, live off-campus either in Shadow Ridge, Shadow Terrace, or Shadow City itself."

"Shadow Terrace?" I'd never heard of that city.

"Yeah, that's the city on the other side of the river. We didn't have a large enough population at first to protect both sides, so the vampires took it over." He shrugged. "The wolves protect our side for Shadow City since all the shifter council members are wolves. The vampires need human blood, and protecting the other side helps them stay under the radar and funnel blood in for the residents."

"Wait..." The thought turned my stomach. "Are you saying you all allow the vampires to kill humans?"

"No." He shook his head. "Not at all. They compel visiting humans to donate blood under the ruse of a local blood bank. They aren't allowed to directly feed from humans since that eventually makes them lose their humanity and can bring the kind of attention we don't want to our area. The whole point is to blend in."

There was so much I didn't know. "So only wolves are on the council?" That seemed surprising with all the races that lived there.

"No, there are twelve representatives. Three of each race," Killian explained. "Three vampires, three angels, three witches, and three wolves who represent all the shifter races."

I mulled that over as we drove down the tree-lined road, straight toward a large brick building that had to be at least a hundred yards long and two stories high. In front was a grassy greenway where a few students were sitting with breakfast and books while others were walking into the building.

As we got closer, the road bore to the right toward a large parking lot that looked mostly full.

This was more along the lines of what I'd been expecting.

Killian pulled into the parking lot and parked underneath a tree. "I have a ten o'clock battle strategy class, so let's haul ass to the coffee shop."

"How far is it?" I didn't want to complain, but these shoes weren't the most comfortable.

"In that building." He nodded to the building beside us. "It's toward the back, so not far. I want to be there to introduce you to the coffee shop manager, Carter. He's one of my pack members, and he owes me for helping him out on his English paper." He got out of the truck.

At least it wasn't across campus.

I turned to open my door and found Killian already there. He opened it and held out a hand to me.

"What are you doing?" I was more than capable of getting out of the truck by myself.

His eyes flicked toward the building. "Remember, we're dating." He took my hand and helped me down. "So I'm treating you like I would a girlfriend."

"Oh, right." That made sense. My irritation eased. "So that begins now?"

"Yeah." He chuckled and interlaced our fingers. "That is the arrangement, right?"

"I know. I forgot." That wasn't smart to admit to him.

He shut the door and guided me in the direction of the building. "Well, let's try not to forget around people, okay?"

He was counting on me. I couldn't let him down. "You've got it." I stepped closer to him, our arms brushing. I hoped I was doing this right, because I'd never dated anyone in my entire life. Watch him go to hold my hand, and I wind up shaking his. There were so many ways I could mess up.

The fact that his presence was comforting but nothing more than that surprised me. He was very good-looking. Probably the most attractive guy I'd ever seen, plus he was kind. Why didn't I find him more desirable?

My skin started buzzing, and I wasn't sure why. Anticipation? Something seemed to tug me toward the building, but maybe it was nerves. Shit had been getting weird lately, so maybe this was my new norm.

The wind blew, lifting my skirt. I managed to use my free hand to catch it before my borrowed panties were revealed to the world. I hated to wear someone else's underwear, but with a dress, I hadn't wanted to chance showing off my kitty. "How many classes do you have today?" I grumbled as I glared at the air around me.

"First off, I'm thinking the wind isn't scared of you." He smiled so wide dimples appeared on both sides of his cheeks. "And I have two—Battle Strategy and Supernatural History. Classes that are expected of me since my pack is responsible for defending Shadow City."

Well aware of the irony, I stared at those dimples. No wonder so many girls fell into bed with him. "And what am I supposed to do while you're busy?" The thought of hanging around all of these supernaturals by myself alarmed me.

"Trust me." He winked.

We walked past a girl who took a quick breath. I turned my head toward her and regretted the decision immediately.

If looks could kill, I'd be dead.

My internal joke fell flat. Death wasn't funny.

"You okay?" he asked.

"That girl is giving me a hateful look." I nodded behind me. "I have no clue what I did to make her dislike me." I sniffed toward each shoulder, wondering if I smelled.

He laughed loudly. "You don't stink, and I hooked up with her last weekend, so that's probably why. I don't want to be tied down, you know?"

"Really?" No wonder she was pissed. If it'd been me, I would've beat the ever-loving shit out of him. "How the hell are we going to get everyone to believe you drastically changed your ways?"

"When you know, you know." He smiled tenderly at me and brushed his fingers against my cheek.

"Save it for everyone else." I wrinkled my nose, trying like hell to hide my laughter.

We got to the large double doors, and he pulled one open.

This time, I knew to wait. When he waved me in, I stepped inside and took in my surroundings. The walls were the standard beige with forest brown tile floor. The hallway that branched off to the left held offices that looked like they were for admissions, financial aid, and all of the various types of administrative departments needed for a college of this size.

In front of me was a back entrance that led to picnic

tables and the river. To the right was a bookstore with an attached coffee shop, and to the immediate left was a cafeteria with indoor seating.

"'This way." Killian took my hand again and led me into Shadow Ridge Coffee.

There was an obvious theme around here.

Inside it looked like a standard coffee shop. There were a few tables that students had already taken over, and in the center were two espresso machines and someone taking orders. The line stretched outside the entrance and into the cafeteria.

Dragging me behind him, Killian went to the front of the line where an attractive guy who had to be close to twenty stood taking orders. His shaggy brown hair hung in his eyes and sweat beaded his forehead. He chewed his bottom lip like it was a piece of gum. The nice fact that he had a deep musky scent that identified him as a wolf shifter made me feel better.

"Carter." Killian leaned his hip against the counter.

"Dude, I don't have time right now." He hit some buttons on the machine and frowned. "It's rush hour, and that bitch Deissy called in sick. Now I have to work the cash register, and a demon lives in it."

"A demon?" I leaned over the counter, but nothing out of the ordinary appeared to be happening. I didn't realize that demons lived on Earth.

"Yes, because it won't work for me." He smacked the buttons like that would make everything better and then paused. He glanced at my and Killian's connected hands. "Uh... this has to be some kind of whacked-out nightmare. You're holding hands with a girl?"

"Well, yeah, but I didn't come here to declare my relationship status. I need a favor." Killian placed an arm loosely around my shoulders. "Dove needs a job, and you owe me one."

"Her name is Dove?" His forehead furrowed.

The girl standing in front crossed her arms and tapped her foot. "Are you going to get my coffee or not?"

Carter's moss-green eyes focused on me. "Do you know how to work a cash register?"

"It shouldn't be hard to figure out." It had buttons with words.

"Then you're hired." He held his hand out. "It's not like I could say no anyway since Killian is my alpha. Give me your ID so I can enter your information and you can get to work."

Shit, I hadn't thought that through. I didn't have anything to give him, and if I left, people would get suspicious. Anyone looking for a job would know to bring their ID with them.

How the hell did I get out of this situation?

CHAPTER SIX

My eyes flicked toward Killian. I was at a loss as to what to say. The fact that I was already relying on him so much was unnerving. I hadn't even known him for twenty-four hours. I hoped my trust wasn't misguided by a desperate attempt to find someone to have my back so I wasn't alone.

Killian sighed exasperatedly. "Man, can we get it to you tomorrow? It's my fault that she doesn't have it at the moment."

"Of course it is, but I don't want any details. There's no telling what you two did to cause that." Carter rolled his eyes. "I'm desperate, so I'm willing to make an exception. But I need it first thing in the morning or no deal."

Thank God. I hadn't expected him to roll over. "So I can start tomorrow?"

"Fuck no." Carter pointed to the wall behind the counter where several black aprons were hanging on a hook mounted in the center. "Get one of those on and get your ass over here. We'll work the line together."

I moved quickly and snatched an apron before he changed his mind.

"All right then." Killian saluted me. "I'll let you get to work. I'll come by after my classes to get you." He kissed my cheek. "See you soon."

My cheeks warmed. I'd never received that kind of attention before, and a few girls in line gawked at his display of affection, making the entire situation even more uncomfortable.

"I like it when you blush." He brushed his pointer finger against my cheek. "But I'll get out of your way."

"Please do." Carter scowled. "I'm pretty sure PDA goes against sanitation rules, not to mention the cat fight that could break out."

"See you." I glared sternly. I didn't want my boss to get pissed at me during my first minute on the clock. Well, I was pretty sure he was my boss since he hired me.

Killian walked out the entrance, and the girl who'd been demanding her latte tilted her head. Her straight, long, mahogany hair fell over her shoulder, contrasting with her fair, unblemished skin. "Did you actually snag Killian?" She leaned over the cash register, and her rose scent hit my nose as her gorgeous dark purple stardust-colored irises focused on me.

She somehow smelled even more pleasant than the flower. She was breathtaking, but I had no clue what kind of supernatural she was. "Snag?"

She flipped her hair over her shoulder and tugged at the edges of her coral sweater, pulling it over her dressy white shirt. "Wow. You're a mindless bimbo like the other girls he's messed around with. And here I was intrigued by you. Obviously, you're not any different and aren't worth talking to." She wrinkled her nose.

What a jerk. I couldn't stand being talked down to. "Wow, that hurt," I said, emphasizing my sarcasm. "I mean a girl yelling at a poor guy who's trying to wait on her is always *super* classy. I really give a flying fuck what she thinks of me."

"Dove!" Carter gasped and his shoulders sagged. "I'm so sorry, Rosemary. She's new—"

"Yeah, I was standing here when that whole exchange went down. I know she's new." She licked her bottom lip and placed a hand on her hip. "But I'm glad you finally hired someone who has the balls to not take any crap." She grinned at me as approval radiated from her. "Do you think you can ring me up better than he can?"

"Of course." Girls like her respected others only when they demanded it. Granted, I wasn't sure how she'd take it here in front of everyone, but I went with my gut. Maybe I wasn't so out of sorts after all.

I sucked in a breath and stared the cash register down. I'd figure out how to work it. Another thing kicking my ass wasn't an option.

THE NEXT TWO hours passed in a blur. After initially struggling with the cash register, I finally conquered the beast, and Carter stopped grumbling about my bad attitude. He was happily helping make the drinks, leaving me alone in front.

We'd been nonstop, but the line was finally dwindling. Every kind of supernatural went to school here; it was a little unnerving. I'd seen almost every kind of shifter, plus vampires and witches. Even several I couldn't identify, which meant that I had never been around that race before.

My guess was that most of the unknown races had been living in Shadow City and were only now integrating back into the world.

I needed to learn more about this city if I was going to survive and stay off the grid.

Something inside me *tugged*, and I looked away from the cash register toward the entrance. The most gorgeous guy I'd ever seen stepped into my view.

His honey-brown hair was slightly longer on top and gelled to sweep to one side. The fluorescent lights of the shop reflected off blond highlights. His golden scruff made his sculpted face perfect. He towered over everyone, standing probably more than half a foot taller than me, and his hunter green polo shirt hugged his body, revealing chiseled abs.

And my heart fell when I noted his arm was wrapped around a girl.

Why in the world was I upset over someone I'd just seen for the first time in my life?

I must have been gawking because his light hazel gaze landed on me. His shirt brought out flecks of green in his irises. He dropped his hand to his side, and the girl pouted her overly done red lips.

Her long, golden blonde hair waved over her tight russet brown crop top. She slid one finger underneath her gold mini skirt, pulling it down a little to reveal more of her stomach. She pretended to stumble in her silver stilettos. "Oh, Griffin." She placed her hands on his chest, using him to steady herself.

They both smelled of musk, alerting me that they were wolf shifters, which further proved that her accident was forced.

He gently pushed her off him and marched past the line

directly to me. A lopsided grin spread across his face. "Hey, you."

"Uh. Hi?" What was he doing up here?

Rubbing his thumb against his bottom lip, he nodded. "I'll take a coffee."

Was this a joke? It had to be. I kept waiting for the punchline, but he looked expectantly at me.

That wasn't how this worked. "The line starts back there." I pointed to where his girlfriend stood, her mouth hanging open.

"It's fine." He glanced at the guy in front of the line next to him, who happened to be another wolf. "Tell her."

"Uh... yeah." The guy averted his eyes, submitting to the asshole.

"The line is back there," I said sternly.

"Dove." Carter rushed over and scowled. "Please forgive her. She's new on the job *and* in town. I'll grab your coffee. Do you want cream?"

The alpha douche leaned toward me and winked. "I only like my cream in one place."

"Ew." Did that actually work for him? "Please stop. God."

"Some confuse me with him, but I assure you, I'm not." He took a step closer to me. "Granted, you'll be calling me that name again before the night—"

I turned away from him and focused on the guy in the front of the line. "What were you saying you wanted again?"

"Hey, I'm talking to you," the gorgeous asshole said as he reached for my arm.

My heart sputtered at the thought of him touching me. I had to rein this in. This guy was clearly a player, and his girlfriend was *not* happy about the scene going down. But I couldn't stop anticipating his touch.

"Dove!" Killian's comforting voice called from the entrance.

My tormentor stilled as Killian walked toward me.

Killian's eyes widened when he looked at the guy. "Hey, you two have already met?"

Wait. This had to be his best friend, Griffin. I almost threw up in my mouth. But Killian had said he slept around, and clearly this guy did too, so maybe it did make sense.

"Us two?" Griffin pointed at me and then back at him. "I was ordering a cup of coffee."

"So you cut the line again?" Killian smirked and nudged over to me, kissing me on my cheek. "This makes the whole first meeting thing easier. This is the girl I was telling you about yesterday."

Griffin frowned as his hands clenched. "Of course, it is." He took a step in my direction, and my traitorous heart picked up its pace.

Did he feel the *tug* too? The thought both thrilled and petrified me.

"You mean the one that you stood Jessica up for?" Griffin's girlfriend said as she sashayed over to us and looped her arm through Griffin's, stopping him from getting closer to me.

"Here's your coffee." Carter hurried back and handed Griffin a cup. "And Dove, maybe you should head out. The line is shorter, and you're making a scene."

"When should I have her here again?" Killian took my hand and pulled me toward him.

A low growl emanated from Griffin as his nostrils flared, but no one but me seemed to notice.

"Tomorrow. She got off to a rough start with Rosemary, of all people, but redeemed herself and did great until

Griffin showed up." Carter held his hand out. "Give me the apron, and be here by nine. That's when things get crazy."

I looked at Killian. I couldn't commit to the time because I'd be relying on him to bring me here.

"She'll be here." Killian unlaced my apron and pulled it over my head. "Thanks, man."

"Please—" Carter placed his palms together, fingertips pointed upward like in prayer "—behave a little better tomorrow."

"Hey, I behaved today." I refused to be pushed around by some pompous student who thought his farts didn't stink, no matter how much I was drawn to him physically.

"That's what I was afraid of." He sighed. "I'll see you tomorrow."

Killian chuckled as he beamed at me. "That's my girl."

The blonde girl arched a perfectly styled eyebrow and held out her hand to me. "I'm Luna. Griffin's girlfriend."

"Friend." Griffin jerked his head in her direction and huffed. "Just friend. How many times do I have to tell you that?"

"Yeah, you made that clear when you hit on Killian's girl, didn't you?" Luna shifted her weight to one leg.

"You hit on her?" Killian grinned and interlaced our fingers.

"God, I hope not." I couldn't tear my gaze away from the sexy douchebag, so I bit out the next words for added measure. "Because if that's his game, it's subpar."

"I wasn't putting forth my best effort." His eyes glowed faintly, making the hazel stand out more as his wolf surged forward. "If I wanted you, you wouldn't be able to deny me."

The problem was I already didn't want to deny him, which meant I had to set clear boundaries more for me than him. "No means no." I placed an arm in front of my body. "Even if you try to force your alpha will on someone."

"I never have or would force anyone." Griffin lifted his chin. "They all come willingly, and some even beg."

Luna cleared her throat and frowned.

"Wow, okay." Killian rolled his shoulders. "We got it. Griffin wasn't hitting on you, and you didn't like the way he came across. I say we start over."

If I didn't feel so indebted to him, I wouldn't have been willing to drop it. But, for him, I would behave. At least for now. "Of course. Anything for you." I managed to pry my attention away from Griffin and turn my focus to him.

"Do you all want to go grab a bite to eat?" Killian gestured to the cafeteria. "I'm starving, and we can beat the lunch crowd."

"Really?" Luna sighed. "Here?"

"Why don't we go off campus to Dick's bar?" Griffin asked as he continued to stare at me. "I could use a beer."

"That sounds a lot better." Luna ran one hand along the top of her breasts. "Daddy has some wolfsbane we can use to lace the drinks too. I'm down for getting tipsy if everyone else is."

"I'm good with that." Killian faced me. "Are you?"

No, but I couldn't be an ass. "Why don't you go? I don't want to interfere with your friends' time."

"I insist," Griffin interjected. "After all, you're my best friend's girl. Clearly, we should get to know each other." He smirked, but there was something sparking dangerously behind his eyes.

He knew he was making me feel uncomfortable.

The asshole.

But the wolf inside me refused to cower. Alpha will and all. That had to be it. It couldn't be that I just wanted to be around him more. "I think I got to know you plenty well the first minute you spoke to me."

"Hey, I thought we were starting fresh." Killian glanced from me to Griffin with his brows furrowed. "That lasted all of ten seconds."

"I have to agree." Luna took my arm and pulled me toward the front of the coffee shop. "We're making a scene here, and it'll be *so* much more *fun* with you there."

The way she said those words made me cringe. Her tone was almost malicious, like she'd enjoyed watching Griffin and me fight. But why would she? I needed to understand what she gained by that.

She led us to the front door, keeping a firm grip on me.

"Dude, what's your problem?" Killian said quietly.

If I didn't have better hearing than most wolves, his voice would have been too low to hear, but with the moon waxing, I could make it out... barely. In a few days, I could've heard them with no problem.

"She was rude to me," Griffin grumbled. "She refused to serve me."

Killian snorted. "That's what all this animosity between you two is about?"

"Don't worry." Griffin sighed. "She's your girl. I'll make nice. After all, it's part of the politician degree that's being forced on me."

"Thank you," Killian said, sounding sincere. "It means a lot. She's important to me. And it's a political science degree."

"They're the same thing." Griffin sighed. "All I'm learning is to be fake and kiss ass."

I could agree with that. I hated politics. Be direct with a caring heart, and the world would be a much better place.

"Is she your fated mate?" Griffin asked with an edge.

"You didn't say a word about her 'til last night, and all of a sudden, you seem kinda shoved up her ass."

"Because I bailed on you last night and then picked her up from the coffee shop?" Killian sounded amused. "That's a bit of a stretch, don't you think? And no, she's not my fated mate. But hey, I may never find mine, and she's gorgeous."

Fated mates were what every supernatural coveted. It was the purest kind of bond, and in my pack, the fated pairs who'd found each other clearly loved their mates uncondi- tionally. That kind of love was breathtaking, and once upon a time, I had wanted that. But now, the pain I felt at losing my pack made me hesitant. If it hurt this much to lose my pack, I couldn't fathom what it'd feel like to lose my fated mate.

"So, where are you from?" Luna gestured to the door, indicating for me to open it for her.

Wow. Entitled much?

But I'd already rocked the boat with Griffin. I should probably shove the pride down and do it. Hating myself, I opened the door for her and gritted my teeth. "North of here."

She smiled brightly as she marched past me, knocking her shoulder into me.

She was declaring war between the two of us. She linked her arm through mine again and yanked me forward, putting more distance between us and the guys.

"I want to be clear with you." She cut her eyes at me. "Griffin is mine. Him hitting on you earlier doesn't make you special. He hits on all the girls who are relatively good-looking."

That was a backhanded compliment. Not only that, but she was also trying to mess with me because it was clear that Griffin wasn't that into her, and she was trying to force it. "I didn't think much of it, but since you brought it up again, maybe I should give him a chance."

She laughed without humor. "Look, you're dating Killian, which is tragic, but whatever. Don't get any funny ideas."

"If he hits on every girl that walks, why do you want him?" One thing silver wolves were good at was reading intent, and hers was all negative. The inkiness of her soul floated off her in waves. She wasn't a good person, and she enjoyed power.

"That's none of your business." She looked forward, her ass swinging with each step, no doubt in case Griffin was watching.

Fair enough. "Look, he's an egotistical asshole. Have at him." Whatever the *tug* was between us, I'd learn to ignore it.

"Oh, you think I was asking for your permission?" She giggled. "I wasn't. I was trying to help you out since Killian seems smitten with you. If we're going to be civil to one another, it's always nice to know the ground rules. I'd hate for you to make a mistake and something tragic to happen."

The air sawed into my lungs at the veiled threat. Maybe this place wasn't safer after all.

CHAPTER SEVEN

K illian climbed into the truck and shut the door. He turned and watched me buckle my seatbelt.

I could feel his scrutiny, and I didn't like it. Dad always did this when he was about to ask a question and wanted to read my body language before, during, and after.

"So..." He tapped his fingers on the center console. "You and Griffin don't seem to like each other. What happened?"

At least, he didn't sugarcoat it. "He told me he likes his cream in only one place. Be glad I had self-control, or his ass would've been on the floor."

"He *did* hit on you." Killian laughed so loud it hurt my ears, his dimples on full display. "That's his favorite coffee shop pickup line, by the way."

Ew. "You'd think after it didn't work the first time, he would've stopped and not continued to embarrass himself."

"You're the first girl it hasn't worked on." Killian turned the ignition and shook his head. "For the first time ever, not only did Griffin get shot down, but I got a girl that he didn't pass over."

"Pass over?" I'd regret asking.

"Everyone wants him over me. Partly due to his role in Shadow City." Killian shrugged like it was no big deal, but his shoulders sagged a little. "So, I usually wind up with the girls he doesn't look at."

"Why in God's name would someone pass you over for him?" Killian was loyal and kind. So much better than the sexy asshole that I refused to think about.

He laughed. "You don't have to sweet-talk me when it's the two of us."

"That's not it at all." He obviously didn't see himself in the right light. "He's arrogant and annoying." I managed to leave *dead sexy* out of the description, but unfortunately, he was that. And I hated that I found him that way.

"You do realize that's how people view me too?" He glanced over his shoulder and reversed out of the parking spot.

The way that girl had stared at me earlier kind of confirmed his point. I'd half expected her to come up and grab my hair for a cat fight. "Maybe, but you haven't acted that way toward me." And I couldn't judge him on anything other than that.

He put the car in drive and headed toward the campus exit. "Don't be too hard on him. Griffin is a good guy. He was there for me and got me through that first year after losing my family. He forced my ass to get out of bed and go for runs. Not only that, but he takes care of his mother, Ulva —she lives alone in this huge condominium since his dad passed—despite him hating being there. He doesn't show that side to anyone, especially not Luna. Thank God."

My feet were killing me, so I slipped off the shoes and rubbed my heels where blisters had formed. They'd heal within a few hours, especially since we'd be sitting down at the restaurant.

"What's wrong?" He glanced at where I was rubbing. "Her shoes don't fit you. Why didn't you tell me?"

"I can make do until I get my first check." I smoothed out the skirt of the dress. "Your sister and I have extremely different tastes." I cringed.

Killian's jaw clenched, but his expression smoothed a moment later. "Let me guess, you're a 'jeans and T-shirt' type of girl."

"Yes." I nodded. "Dresses and skirts are so restricting. What happens when you need to fight? Trying to make sure I didn't flash my panties at my opponent would hinder my abilities."

"First off, do you get into fights often?" He leaned against his door. "And second, even if you did, would you be focused on flashing as opposed to kicking ass?"

"Part of our training regimen was fighting every day, usually several times. And, yes, I would care if anyone saw my panties." Dad had taught me to be conservative and dress appropriately for battle. It could happen at any time.

He'd been right about that.

"Are you a—" He paused and faced me. He scanned my face and his mouth gaped. "You're a virgin, aren't you?"

Most supernaturals were pretty open about enjoying sex as much as they pleased, so the fact that I hadn't slept with someone probably was shocking. It was that, with my position intimidating everyone, I'd never found someone I clicked with, and I didn't want to have sex for the sake of having sex. "You make it sound like a bad thing."

"Hell, no." He perused my body. "It makes you hotter. How is that possible?"

"Well, you see, I keep my legs closed nice and tight." What kind of question was that? Plus, his attention was making me uncomfortable.

"You are a breath of fresh air." He focused back on the road. "Within the first few seconds of me meeting you, you elbowed my stomach and broke my nose. And you say whatever you think with no hidden agenda. It's nice."

I'd forgotten about his nose. He hadn't said much of anything about it when we'd gotten back to his place, but now that he'd pointed it out, I could see that it was a little crooked. His bones had healed that way. "I'm so sorry. We should've tried to straighten it."

"Are you kidding me?" He flexed the arm nearest me, making his bicep muscle bulge. "You've officially made me sexier. No girl will be able to let me walk by."

"Remember, we're exclusive." I teased him. "I will cut your pecker off if you cheat and make me look like a fool."

"I don't think I'm scared." He chuckled. "You probably wouldn't know what to do with it once it was unleashed."

"Oh, ha. Ha." He was right, but I'd never admit that to him.

We drove into the bustling downtown again, and he pulled into a small parking lot next to a brick building that stood separate from the others. A huge sign on the front read Dick's Bar.

"Really?" I gestured to the name. "That's the name of the bar? Let me guess. Griffin named it."

"Believe it or not, that's Luna's dad's name, and he owns the bar." He pulled into a spot next to a black Navigator on my side. "And want to hear their last name? It makes it even more epic."

I was officially afraid. Not of my life being in danger but that I would regret playing into Killian's hand. "What?"

"Harding." He cracked up. "His name is Dick Harding."

I snorted. "No. Tell me he goes by Richard."

"He does not." He opened the door and winked. "'That's

what makes it even more epic. Just a heads up, he's Griffin's Beta."

That was good to know.

I watched Killian move toward me, but my door opened, startling me. I'd been so caught up in Killian's and my conversation that I hadn't noticed Griffin come up to my car door and open it. I inhaled as that weird *tug* clenched inside my chest.

Griffin leaned over me and unbuckled my seatbelt. "Are you two having a good time?"

His fingers brushed my arm, and my skin buzzed. I inhaled deeply, smelling his musky myrrh and leather scent. My body warmed. What in the hell was going on between us? Maybe it was lust. That was all it could be.

Nope. Not happening. Shutting that down.

I grabbed his arm and pulled it away from me as the seat belt slid off. "Thanks, but I've got it."

His hazel eyes appeared to glow, making my palms sweaty. "Hey, you're my best friend's girl. I gotta make sure you're taken care of."

"Dude, back off," Killian said as he pushed Griffin away. "She's mine. Go find yourself another one-night stand."

Griffin leaned against the Navigator as I slipped from the car and took Killian's hand. I not only was emphasizing to him that I was with Killian but begrudgingly doing it to remind myself.

A frown formed on Griffin's face, and his shoulders drooped, making me feel guilty for holding Killian's hand. I hadn't done anything wrong, but I couldn't shake the feeling.

High heels clacked on the cement as Luna's overly ripe scent announced her arrival. She stuck out her bottom lip and glared at Griffin. "What the hell, Griff? You left me. I thought we were riding together."

"Sorry." His attention stayed on me. "I've got some things to do after this, so you needed to drive separately."

"You could've told me that, and besides, I'm not busy." She brushed a hand on his shoulder. "I can go with you."

My body tensed at her proximity to him, but I pushed the sensation away. He could let whoever he wanted to touch him.

Griffin removed her hand. "Nope, you can't."

The way he dismissed her made me way too happy.

"So, while you two figure out your plans, Dove and I are heading inside." Killian wrapped an arm around my waist and nudged me toward the entrance.

A low growl emanated from behind me, and I forced myself to keep my eyes forward and not look back to see what Griffin was upset about. If I confirmed he felt whatever this *tug* was between us, it would only make it harder for me to keep my distance.

"Don't you dare walk away from me," Luna yelled as her heels click-clacked after him. "You're going to talk to me. What the hell is your problem?"

"Hurry, let's get out of here," Killian whispered close to my ear.

Griffin sighed. "Can you stop being a drama queen?"

Oh, that wasn't smart. Calling a woman a drama queen was equivalent to calling a crazy person... well... crazy.

"I'll show you drama queen," Luna whispered threateningly.

Killian and I entered the building. The bar was one large open square with a cherry wood bar in the middle of the wall to the right. Three people were working behind the counter, and it looked like they had several beers on tap along with a cabinet full of wines and liquors. Cups of varying sizes were shelved below the cabinets. Stools lined the bar, and about twenty round tables were scattered around the main floor. The walls were made of varying neutral colors of brick with booths set against them. Televisions hung in every corner of the room, but they weren't blaring.

"I can actually hear myself think." This wasn't as bad as I'd expected. Between the tolerable noise level and lack of smoke, eating here wouldn't be that bad. Well, if Griffin and Luna weren't going to be joining us.

"This is a bar owned by wolf shifters in a mostly supernatural town." Killian bumped his shoulder into mine. "None of us like loud noises."

Fair point.

A beautiful sandy-blonde-haired girl headed in our direction. She wore a white button-down shirt and gray slacks that matched her eyes. She was a few inches shorter than me, but she walked with such poise that she appeared taller. Her hair was pulled back into a low ponytail with tendrils framing her face. "Hey, Killian." She smirked when her attention landed on me. "Who's this?"

"Sierra, this is Dove." He kissed my cheek and pulled back, gesturing to the girl. "Dove, this is Sierra. One of the few girls in town who knows how to handle both Griffin's and my asses."

"Handle?" She laughed. "I don't know if I would go that far, but I gotta say, you've never been one to take a girl out the day after a night of passion."

"She's different." He wrapped an arm around my waist. "She's tamed my wild ways."

"A girl after my own heart." Sierra leaned toward me.

"You'll have to tell me your secret skills later, but for now, is it just the two of you?"

"No, unfortunately, Griffin and the devil incarnate will be joining us momentarily." Killian shivered. "Did you bring the holy water?"

"Between her and her dad, I always have extra on hand."

"Is her dad as bad as she is?" I couldn't imagine that.

Sierra grabbed four laminated menus and rolled her eyes. "He's worse in a different way. He wants everything to be perfect, but he's super nice. Luna demands all the attention. She's had her sights set on Griffin since she was a kid."

"That long?" I could kind of see it.

"Yes, that long." She waved for us to follow her. "Where are you from? I haven't seen you around."

"Oh, that's because I'm new." I had no clue what else to say. I didn't want to tell her how I got here, and I couldn't lie, mainly because she'd know. "Killian found me, and the rest is history."

"He tries to be a player like Griffin, but he could never quite pull it off." She stopped at a booth and turned to Killian, squishing his cheeks. "And now he has a girlfriend. My little buddy is growing up."

"You two act like brother and sister." I slid into the booth and scooted over to the wall.

Killian got in beside me and took my hand, placing it on the table. "We pretty much are. She was my sister's best friend. Sierra is my age, but she clicked with my younger sister because they had the same maturity level."

"Yup, Olive was way more mature than Killian." Sierra jutted her hip. "If she was here, she'd be kicking his ass into gear. Maybe you could do that job since he won't listen to anyone else."

"Olive had a way," Killian said with longing.

The *tug* pulled at me once again, and my attention went to the front door as it opened and Luna and Griffin marched inside. They radiated tension and avoided looking in each other's direction.

A man entered and walked around them, taking a seat at the end of the bar near a small hallway that had an exit sign.

Sierra frowned and blew out a breath. "I still miss her so much."

"Oh, God." Luna sighed as she slid into the booth on the opposite side. "Every time Sierra serves us, we have to talk about Olive. She's dead; it sucks. We've got to move on."

"So, when you die, you want your friends or family to never think of you?" I stared the entitled brat down. "We should roll our eyes and tell everyone to move on?"

One side of Griffin's lips tugged upward until Killian wrapped an arm around my shoulders. The smile slipped from Griffin's face, and he glared at us.

"I will take every opportunity to talk about my sister and celebrate her life and her friends." Killian wrinkled his nose. "If that bothers you, you can go sit at a different table."

"You are kind of being a bitch," Griffin said as he slid in next to her. "Don't take out your anger at me on them."

"Fine." Luna crossed her arms, her body language making it clear she wouldn't be apologizing. The tension grew thick between us.

The image of my pack members, bloody and dying, popped into my mind. My eyes burned with unshed tears, and I choked back a sob. I cleared my throat, desperate for my words to sound normal. "I need to run to the bathroom." I nudged Killian's arm, making sure he heard me.

"Oh, yeah." Killian stood.

I slid out and glanced around the room, looking for a restroom sign.

"It's over there before the back exit." Sierra pointed toward the small hallway I'd noticed earlier. "There's a men's and women's bathroom on either side of the hall."

"Thanks." I hurried in that direction, desperate for some time alone to compose myself. I didn't want to break down in front of Griffin and definitely not Luna. I didn't want either one of them to think I was weak.

"Is she okay?" Sierra asked the table.

Killian cleared his throat. "I'm sure she's fine."

The hallway was dark, not that it mattered with my wolf eyes, and longer than it looked. The women's bathroom was the door on the right. A few tears spilled over and trailed down my cheeks.

Dammit. My numbness was wearing off fast. Focused on getting into the bathroom to hide my imminent breakdown, I pushed the door open.

A calloused hand grabbed my arm and yanked. Another arm snaked around my neck and placed a knife against my throat.

"One sound, and I'll slit your throat," a deep voice hissed.

CHAPTER EIGHT

He nudged the knife deeper into my skin. Warm liquid trickled down my neck as the copper scent of blood hit my nose. This prick was enjoying himself.

"What do you want?" I asked, trying to keep my fear at bay, hoping to learn something—anything—about why I was such a target.

"Absolutely nothing." He chuckled darkly, "Other than you need to move to the exit now." He pushed me forward, and I stumbled, causing the knife to dig a little deeper.

Asshole.

I'd rather die right there than leave. With a knife to my neck, there was only one way this could go.

Keeping my arms close to my body, I raised my hands toward his knife arm and relaxed my body into his chest. He loosened his hold, and I grabbed his wrist with both of my hands and pulled down and away from my neck.

"What—" He hissed.

His hold slackened and I slipped under his arm, keeping my grip firm on his wrist. When I broke free, I shoved the hand holding the knife back at him so the blade cut into his side.

"You stupid bitch," he yelled as he tried to recapture me with his free arm. Using his slumped angle to my advantage, I kicked his face and twisted his wrist, manipulating a pressure point by his thumb to make him release the hold on the knife. He stumbled back, and I kicked the knife away.

"Dove!" Killian yelled, but I didn't have time to answer him.

This guy wouldn't go down without a fight.

As he stood and faced me, I could see the spot where my foot had connected with his jaw. For the first time, I got a good view of him.

It was the guy who'd entered the bar behind Griffin and Luna.

His hair was dyed an awful ash blond, except for the dark brown sides. His long beard hit the top of the collar of his black shirt, connecting with the chest hair that spilled there. His hairy arms were almost as thick as his beard. I already suspected he was a bear shifter, and his grassy scent confirmed it.

"You're going to pay for that." He snatched my arm again and dragged me toward the exit.

Bear shifters were strong, but their arrogance worked against them.

"Let her go," Griffin commanded, alpha will lacing his words.

He was a fucking moron if he thought that would work on a bear, and massively egotistical if he thought that the bear would listen to him in the first place. He had no authority over them.

Confirming my suspicions, the bear shifter didn't loosen

his grip on me. Instead, he tightened it and dragged me harder.

I might not have had a knife to my neck anymore, but that didn't mean I wasn't at risk of being taken. Doing the first thing that came to mind, I stuck my fingers into one of his knife wounds and made my hands like claws, breaking through fat and muscle. The wound needed to get worse, so I dug my fingers in hard, trying to get his brain to register the pain. With all the adrenaline pumping through his body, he probably hadn't even noticed he'd been stabbed.

He swung his free hand, aiming for my face, but I easily blocked it.

Dad had been right all along. If we didn't know how to protect ourselves, we were screwed. I wished I could take back all of those times I talked smack about him or complained.

Because of him, I still stood here, surviving.

As I straightened, I pulled my hands out of his side and round-kicked the asshole in the stomach. He fell against the brick wall.

"We can take it from here," Killian said as he got closer.

Oh, hell no. This was all me.

I scooped the knife from the floor as Killian and Griffin reached me. They grabbed the guy by the arms as I ran behind the bear shifter and placed the knife against his throat. I leaned in and saw blood well from beneath the blade. "Who are you, and what do you want from me?"

"Go to hell." He spat in my face.

Nope, that wasn't acceptable. I elbowed him hard in the temple, knocking him unconscious, and let him crumble to the floor. "Stupid prick."

"Uh. Wow." Killian snorted as he and Griffin released the guy, letting him drop to the floor.

I used the sleeve of my dress to wipe away the spittle. I wanted a shower *now*.

Sierra gasped, "She's freaking badass."

"Badass?" Luna scoffed. "Men are supposed to be the protectors, not us. That was extremely unladylike."

Oh, wow. Her beliefs were archaic. Good thing I wasn't raised that way, or I'd be captured or dead by now.

"Hey, are you hurt?" Killian rushed over to examine me.

"Look at her neck," Griffin said through clenched teeth. "The bastard cut her. I'm going to make him pay."

"I'm fine." Both of them were being a little too much. "Besides, I knocked him out cold. Everything will be okay, but I want answers."

I glanced down at my dress and cringed. Not only was I wearing this godforsaken thing, but I didn't have my knife on me because of the outfit. I needed better clothes and pronto.

Footsteps pounded in our direction. "What's going on here?" a deep, raspy voice asked.

"Daddy!" Luna sounded relieved. "A man attacked Dove."

So good ol' Dick Harding was here.

"Dove?" A tall man stepped into the hallway, and his ebony eyes landed on me. He ran a hand through his shortish salt and pepper hair. A frown marred his chiseled face, which was covered by dark brown scruff. "You're new in town."

"Yup." He was more focused on me being new here than the guy lying on the floor? That was a bit strange. "I am."

"I swear, Griffin." Dick looked past me to the bear shifter and shook his head. "We've got to do something about this. Obviously, people are growing more wary of letting residents out of Shadow City, and now you're trying to get me to promote letting people in. That's such a horrible idea for this reason here. Yet another attack targeting wolves."

"There's nothing we can do about it even if I wanted to undo Dad's decision." Griffin kept his attention on me. "The entire council voted, and there was a majority."

My brain struggled to catch up. Nothing they were saying made sense. "You're part of a council?"

"Yes, he is," Luna said and stepped over, placing a hand on Griffin's shoulder. "He's the alpha of Shadow City."

Laughter almost bubbled out of me. This had to be some sort of sick joke. From what I'd seen, he was more interested in getting into various women's pants than being a leader. Maybe his goal was to be a lead douchebag?

Griffin stepped away from Luna, making her hand fall. He cleared his throat. "My dad was the alpha, and he passed away right before the college was built. The alpha power and title fell to me, but Dick has gracefully stepped forward to help lead the city while I attend college and get my priorities in order."

Things clicked into place, and I groaned. I hadn't realized that I'd been holding out hope that Shadow City's new alpha would be my ally. Griffin wouldn't help me. At least, I understood why Luna wanted him and was willing to do whatever it took to lock him down. Hell, almost no one would turn him down. From what Dad said, the city had become the home of some of the strongest supernaturals he'd ever seen, and Atticus had been a beacon of power. If that was the case, that meant that Griffin was one of the most powerful wolves in the world, and snagging him would set his mate up for life.

Killian squatted next to the bear shifter and dug through his pockets. "He has no ID on him or anything."

"That's consistent. It has to be so no one can identify the

attackers if something goes wrong." Dick sighed, but it seemed...off.

What he said had merit, but for some reason, I didn't buy it. This bear was cocky. He'd honestly thought he had me. He wouldn't think to leave his stuff in his car or wherever, so there had to be another reason he carried no ID. I kept my mouth shut, though, since I wasn't alone with Killian.

"Harold." Dick faced the front of the restaurant and clapped. "Take this jackass who attacked this poor girl to Shadow City jail. He's been roughed up enough, so try not to injure him much more. We need him to be able to talk."

A dark olive wolf shifter about Killian's height appeared and walked past us but avoided eye contact. He bent down, picked up the injured bear, and headed straight out the exit door.

He was gone within seconds like he couldn't stand to be near us or was scared. So strange.

"I'm impressed that you handled him without getting injured." Dick tightened his black tie as he addressed Killian and Griffin, ignoring my presence. "And thank God there are no other customers. That could've been a publicity nightmare."

"Actually, Dove took the guy out on her own." Sierra smirked and gestured to me. "Griffin and Killian didn't make it in time."

"Are you serious?" Dick's gaze landed on me, making my skin crawl. "That's *interesting.*"

His negative energy nearly stole my breath. But I couldn't afford to alert him to that little fact. Dad had told me that at some point in my life, I'd meet someone truly evil. And that I couldn't let on that I could sense their darkness because it was a trait only silver wolves had. If I gave away my reaction, I could put not only myself in danger but the people I cared about. Granted, at this time, the total of people I cared about had dwindled to one—Killian. But I had to continue to play the game until I had a royal flush. Only then could I reveal my hand. "What can I say?" I forced my words to sound light, and I smiled. If my gut hadn't warned me, I would've thought he was concerned. "I believe that everyone should know how to protect themselves. Had I not been trained, this situation could've gone an extremely different way."

"So true." He smiled. "Even though men are normally the guards, not the women."

My skin crawled from his creepy-ass smile. Not only that, but he'd chastised me yet somehow managed to make it not sound too judgy. So he was the worst kind of villain—a manipulator—which meant Killian and Griffin were clueless. "In this particular instance, it's a good thing I didn't need a man, or he would've had me out the door." I refused to cower like Dick wanted.

Something unreadable crossed Dick's face before his features smoothed back into place. "Well, I should probably get back to Shadow City. I'd planned on working the books here for a little while today, but that obviously won't be happening."

"I'll go with you," Griffin said as his forehead lined. He scanned me before looking at Killian. "And why don't you take her somewhere safe?" His voice held concern, which shocked me.

"That's a good idea." Killian wrapped an arm around my shoulders and gestured to the exit. "Do you mind if we leave this way?"

"Sure." Dick waved him off, but his shoulders tensed. He turned to Griffin. "Stay here with Luna and have lunch. I can handle the attacker."

"No, I'll go with you." Griffin narrowed his eyes. "Technically, it's my place, not yours. And he attacked my best friend's g—" He cut off like he couldn't say the word and inhaled sharply. "Dove. He attacked Dove right in front of us. That's equivalent to him giving me the middle finger. I want to hear what he has to say."

"But—" Dick started.

Luna touched her dad's arm. "It's a good thing he wants—"

He cut her off with a glare. "Obviously, I can't tell you no, but I think it would be more prudent for you to stay here and enjoy a meal."

Griffin pursed his lips as he considered Dick's words.

"Yes." Dick blatantly didn't want Griffin to go with him, to the point where he was openly discouraging it. "Having lunch is *so* much more important than attending to alpha duties," I said sweetly as I smiled and batted my eyelashes.

"Don't worry, I'm not ready to step in permanently." Griffin straightened. "But like I said, he attacked her right in front of me, almost like a dare. One day, I will take back the role full time, and I need to show everyone I won't take any bullshit."

"Come on." Killian took my hand and opened the back door. "We'll see you guys later."

I let him pull me out the door, but I didn't want to leave. Dick was attempting to make Griffin stand down, and for whatever reason, Griffin had almost allowed it. If I hadn't butted in, I had a feeling he would have lost his nerve. But if Griffin was the true alpha and he wanted to be part of the interrogation, it wasn't Dick's place to tell him no or discourage him.

"You okay?" Killian asked, leading me to his truck.

"Yeah, why?" I focused on Killian. Everything inside me was telling me to go back to Griffin, which I didn't understand. The sensation *tugged* and itched inside me almost to the point of being overwhelming. He had some sort of hold on me, and I didn't like it one bit.

"Let's see, you went up against Dick." He chuckled. "And you were attacked."

"What is Dick's problem?" I tried to sound casual, but I desperately wanted to know.

"Well, he hates a woman talking back to him, but he's a good guy other than that." Killian opened the passenger door. "When Atticus died, the entire wolf pack in Shadow City landed on Griffin's shoulders. He was seventeen. My pack is large, around eight hundred wolves, but he's alpha, not only over the six hundred who live in Shadow City— but he also represents the over fifteen hundred various shifters who live outside. Not only did all the responsibility land on him, but he was grieving for his father while still learning to be a man, just like me. Dick offered to be his proxy. He's taken on a lot of the alpha responsibilities to let Griffin have a semi-normal college experience before Dick hands the reins back to him. That's why Griffin is majoring in political science, preparing for his inevitable role."

So that was the angle the older man was working. I had a gut feeling he had no intention of handing the power back to Griffin. "Is Griffin not your alpha too?" If Killian's pack were the ones protecting the city, it'd make sense that they were connected.

He chuckled. "No. With us living outside, we have our own pack. It works better that way. Besides, if we didn't, then we'd have to get approval from the council for any decisions we—or rather, I—make. It's easiest to stay separate."

"I see. And why didn't you tell me who Griffin was?" That kind of burned, but I didn't have a right to be upset. We'd known each other for only a day, and I had a ton of secrets that I hadn't shared with him. I slid into my seat.

"Because Griffin would rather pretend no one knows, though that's truly impossible." He pulled at his ear. I realized it was a sign that he was uncomfortable. "That kind of role isn't one you can hide from."

"What's going on with the attacks? It sounded like there was more to the bear shifter attacking me today." Maybe today's attack on me was coincidental, but that seemed convenient. Something about the whole thing bothered me.

Killian tapped his fingers on the steering wheel. "Ever since Shadow City began to open back up and the college was built, there's been at least one attack a month on wolves. We think it's because Atticus was the one who headed the charge." He shrugged. "Either way, your best bet is to stick with me, especially since you've been attacked twice in two days."

"I thought Shadow City was a place of refuge. How did it become so volatile?" That was the missing piece that I couldn't get a handle on.

"From what Griffin had told me one drunken night, that had been the intent, but they started recruiting powerful beings and approving only the strongest to move there before the border shut down." He shrugged. "I didn't push for more information, but essentially, only the strongest of the races were allowed into the city."

So much hidden history. But it wasn't my problem. I had something more pressing on my mind. "I need clothes."

I lifted the skirt material. "This isn't cutting it. I need jeans so I can carry my knife around. I hate to ask, but can you cover me until I get my first paycheck?"

"Normally, I would argue with you, but after today, I won't." He pouted. "So I guess that means I'm taking you shopping."

THE REST of the day flew by, despite me looking over my shoulder at all times, expecting to be jumped again. I'd gotten two pairs of jeans, a few shirts, a pair of tennis shoes, and boots at a local thrift store, so tomorrow I'd feel more like myself.

Once my new-to-me stuff was washed, I put it away and then paced around the small bedroom. It was almost eleven at night, and I was restless. My wolf was edgy, not having a pack, and that damn *tug* was working at me again. I'd been waiting for Killian to settle in for the night so I could head out to the backyard and stand in the moonlight for a few minutes. The moon always seemed to soothe my soul and spoke to my wolf in a way that was almost inexplicable. It wasn't nearly as effective as running in animal form, but it would help ease the turmoil brimming within.

As quietly as possible, I opened my door and creeped out to the back porch. Low mumblings from the television from Killian's room informed me he was already in bed. My heart slowed as a sense of calm settled over me. I needed to be alone. He and I had been together all day, and even though I enjoyed his company, I needed space to function properly.

I slipped down the brick steps and around the concrete pool area until my feet touched the grass on the side of the yard. I lifted my face to the moon, feeling a little bit of its power wash over me. Even though it was a trickle compared to a full moon, it was enough to make my blood buzz.

That was when I heard the snap of a branch. I tensed.

I wasn't alone.

CHAPTER NINE

I spun on my heels and faced the direction of the white house next door. The scent of leather and myrrh filled my nose, and the *tug* from earlier reappeared.

Griffin was near.

Dammit. I came out here for peace, and the douchebag showed up here. Maybe he came for a swim. Either way, I had to stay away from him. For some reason, he grated on my nerves by being in close proximity. The fact that I was drawn to his playboy ways pissed me off even more.

No self-respecting girl would want someone like him. And I refused to become another notch in his belt, even if I would love to know how his lips tasted.

That was another reason I didn't need to be around him. I would never taste his lips. Ever.

Hoping he hadn't seen me, I turned to go back inside.

"What are you doing out here alone?" he asked as he stepped from the tree line.

I scowled at him. "Minding my own business, unlike you." I wished there was a privacy fence around the pool so

I could've hidden, but shifters instinctively knew how to swim, so drowning wasn't a hazard.

"Noted." He shoved his hands into his pockets and stopped about five feet away from me. He still had on the same clothes from this afternoon, but he looked a little worse for wear. "You kicked that bear shifter's ass. But I wouldn't get too cocky. You probably couldn't do it again."

"Why, because I'm a girl?" Malice dripped from each word.

Griffin chuckled. "The guy wasn't expecting you to fight back, so you had the element of surprise."

What an arrogant bastard. Granted, I already knew that about him from earlier, but his smugness seemed to get worse each time I saw him, and that had been only twice so far. What would happen next time? Maybe he'd try to prove his point by tossing me in front of a car.

"We could fight now." I'd kick his ass, and that would be the end of it.

Hopefully.

"You think you could take me?" He touched his chest with a huge-ass smirk. His eyes flicked to my mouth, and I licked my lips in response.

Agh, I had to stop. I squared my shoulders and lifted my chin. "I know I can." Especially with the moon shining on me, I could kick his ass with my eyes closed.

"You want to shift into our wolves?" He grabbed the hem of his shirt, ready to remove it.

That was a big fat no. If I shifted, he'd probably know what I was. "Nope, I don't need my animal to make you scream like a girl."

"Well, all right then." He charged at me without warning, fighting dirty.

I wasn't surprised. He moved to wrap his arm around

my waist, and I spun to the right out of his reach. He ran past me and almost fell since he had planned on my body to stop his momentum.

He huffed and faced me as his hazel eyes glowed. "You were lucky."

"You keep saying that." I couldn't help but antagonize him. His first move told me everything I needed to know about him as a fighter. He was strong, but he relied on his strength to win. Besides that, he had no form, no fighting technique, and bad general awareness of how to move. Maybe Shadow City had gotten spoiled since they had guards. This alpha was focused more on political studies and alliances than maneuvers, though I imagined with the proper training, he could be a force on the battlefield.

Rolling his shoulders, he stretched his neck side to side like that would make a difference.

I leaned back on my feet like I didn't have a care in the world. I enjoyed goading him. My body warmed, but I pretended it was from the brawl and not due to the handsome man standing in front of me.

"For what it's worth, I was trying to go easy on you, but not anymore." He shook his hands out at his sides and wiggled. "It's on." He lunged at me, dropping as he kicked out one of his feet with the intent to make me fall.

Wanting to end this, I let the moon charge through my blood and jumped over his leg. I landed behind him and dropped my elbow so that it touched the back of his neck and shoulder but didn't press down hard. "If I wanted to, I could knock you out. You still think I was only lucky earlier?"

He turned, and his chest brushed my side.

Goosebumps spread all over me as my body sizzled. *It has to be the moon*, I lied to myself. But the lie was pointless.

This strange feeling had to do with the sexy guy right in front of me. If I didn't know any better, I'd think he was my fated mate. But a jerk like him *couldn't* be that.

His head lowered to mine, and I didn't want to move. Something coursed between us and made my head fuzzy.

That was what I needed to snap out of whatever spell was captivating us. I took three large steps away from him. The warmth vanished. "What are you doing here?"

"I went for a slow run and was heading back home." He nodded to the white house next door.

His words didn't make sense for a moment. "Wait, you're Killian's neighbor?"

"Right next door." He gestured to the house with all the beer cans littering the yard. "Did your *boyfriend* fail to mention that? I've lived next door to him for two years now."

"Why would he?" Normally men who had overinflated egos were short by shifter standards, so with Griffin's height, I wasn't sure what his excuse might be. Maybe small-dick syndrome. My gaze dropped to his crotch, and I could see the outline in his blue jeans.

No small dick. Maybe insecurity then.

"Because I'm his best friend." He scoffed like that should be obvious. "And we've been inseparable since I left Shadow City."

"Are you sure?" I tilted my head and shrugged. "Because it seems like you're busier hanging out with Luna and her daddy than trying to be a friend to Killian."

"Aw." He chuckled. "It's cute that you're so concerned."

He was enjoying getting under my skin. I wanted to snap back at him, but I'd already said and done too much. I'd come out here to be alone and calm myself. Fighting with him had resulted in the complete opposite.

The time had come for me to take control. I took a few

steps toward Killian's house, determined to leave his ass behind.

"Dove." He sighed and caught up then stepped in front of me. "Give me a moment, please."

Wow, he was being nice...except for blocking me. "You have one minute."

A growl emanated from his chest at my demand, but his eyes softened. "I want to know how you really are."

The concern in his voice caught me off guard. I didn't like him sounding like a nice guy, especially when I got confused vibes from him. There was no evil inside him, which proved that he was a good person, unlike Luna and Dick. Once again, I was thankful for that perk of being a silver wolf—being able to sense someone's true intent. Hating him wasn't possible, despite him getting under my skin. That was why I needed him to be the douchebag from a few minutes ago. "I'm fine." The awful odor of a lie wafted off me.

"You're trying to lie to me?" He coughed and waved a hand in front of his nose. "Do you think I can't smell it or something?"

Man, I hated that he had me there. "The words came out."

And now I didn't have any of them. The hole in my heart ripped open even more. So far, my lone wolf status hadn't fractured me mentally, but the restlessness was a sign of that beginning. I needed to figure out my next steps, which should involve finding another pack, but I couldn't take the risk. At least, not right then. As soon as I joined one, the link would alert them all that I was different than a normal wolf.

Griffin's fingers brushed my arm. "Hey, are you okay? It's like you're somewhere else."

"Yeah, sorry." I would work harder to hold myself together. I couldn't break down, especially in front of him. "And I'll be fine." I internally cringed, waiting for the smell of a lie to reek again, but reassuringly, the air stayed fresh. I did believe that.

Strange.

I hadn't expected to.

"What can I do to make it better?" He inched closer to me. "I want to make things easier for you."

My body betrayed me, and I leaned toward him. I had to forget about his touch, smell, and proximity. "Tell me what you learned from the bear shifter." There. Even if he did affect me, I'd managed to keep our conversation strictly business.

"Well, that was a clusterfuck." His jaw clenched, and his hand dropped as he looked up at the night sky.

Wow, helpful. "Care to expand on that?"

Griffin met my stare. "I came over to tell Killian what happened, and I heard you two eating dinner together."

I studied him, at a loss. "Why didn't you knock?" He didn't seem like the type who would care if we were eating dinner. He'd barge on in.

"I expected him to be alone," he said tightly. "So I was waiting for you to leave, but here you are in the backyard in your pajamas. Are you staying with him?"

"A reminder, I was the one who was attacked, not him." I gestured to the house. "And how is my staying here any of your damn business?"

"It's not." He lifted his hands. "I was curious. And I wanted to talk only to him because I was trying not to see you."

His words stung, which made me even angrier. He shouldn't have this much of an effect on me. In fact, I should have been ecstatic that he didn't want to see me, but the fact that the air didn't smell told me all I needed to know. "Then why did you start talking to me?" If he didn't want to be around me, then he shouldn't have said anything in the first place. "I was about to go inside, and you wouldn't have been forced to have this conversation."

"Because I thought about it, and I figured you should know too." He blew out a breath and narrowed his eyes.

Wanting to get back to the actual point, I crossed my arms. "Then tell me—what happened with the bear shifter?"

"There isn't much to tell." Griffin ran a hand through his gelled hair, messing it up.

I grimaced. He was somehow even more breathtaking.

But I refused to be distracted. No good would come from it. "Well then, this should be a very short conversation," I snapped. One minute, I was trying to be nice to him, and the next, I was angry. My emotions had become a yo-yo, and I didn't know why.

"Remember how that guy who works for Dick—Harold —was taking the bear shifter to the Shadow City jail?" he asked.

"Yup." Maybe if I was brief, he would get to the point faster.

"The bear shifter somehow knocked him unconscious and got away." He clenched his hands into fists. "Which means we have no leads to whether he was the only person in on the attack or if it was a calculated move organized by others. Either way, the asshole is somewhere out here again."

"Wasn't he cuffed?" Surely the guy wouldn't have put the bear in the back of a car unrestrained.

Griffin laughed without humor. "Actually, he wasn't. Harold tied him up with a rope, but the bear shifter pretended to be unconscious and bit through it. He attacked Harold, making him drive off the bridge that leads to Shadow City."

"A bridge?" I hadn't seen more than downtown Shadow Ridge and the university, so I had no clue how many ways there were to enter Shadow City.

He waved his hand in a circular motion. "The river surrounds a large island that Shadow City is built on. The bridge leads to the gate to enter. Witches have spelled the city so that the Tennessee River around it appears narrower than it really is, which is why there isn't a lot of river traffic through here." He rolled his eyes. "Luckily, Harold came to before the car filled with water, but the bear shifter was already gone. His scent was untraceable. I'm sorry you got thrown into this mess. He attacked you because you were with me. They're trying to scare me so I'll try to shut the borders again."

"Then why were you out here alone?" If the bear could be anywhere, it made sense that he might try to attack me again, but we didn't know if I was the target or the most convenient wolf body at the time.

"You were too." Griffin pointed at me. "So, I think that's a little hypocritical."

"I thought he was in jail." In all fairness, if I'd known he'd escaped, my first instinct would have been to track his ass down. But I needed to stay put for a little while longer. I didn't need my hunters finding me, much as I didn't want anyone else suffering an attack. "What's your excuse?"

"My excuse isn't a good one." He closed the distance between us again, and he was so close his minty breath hit my face.

My breathing quickened, almost matching the racing

beat of my heart. "I didn't ask if it was a good one. I asked what it was."

"I wanted to make sure that the bear didn't come looking for you. I was going to ask Killian where you lived. When I realized you were here, I was planning to follow you home." He sighed as if what he said next pained him to admit. "Seeing you hurt like that earlier almost made me go insane."

His words threatened to tear down my walls, but this couldn't happen. Whatever *this* was. "I'm with Killian." It helped that we'd agreed to be exclusive, so this wasn't a lie. Besides, Killian had helped me, and I couldn't let my inconvenient reaction to some hot guy screw up my relationship with the only friend I had.

"Yeah, I'm well aware." A vein between his brows bulged. "Thanks for the reminder."

"What the hell is your problem?" I didn't know what was happening between us. Lust? Would having sex with him get rid of this energy? *Absolutely not.* No way would my first time be with some playboy who got his rocks off by talking about his cream and where he liked it placed.

"Nothing," he said a little too loudly. "Nothing at all. I mean, I'm ready for him to get over his feelings for you and kick your ass to the curb."

"Says the douchebag who hit on me in front of the girl who's trying to manipulate him into settling down." If he wanted to hurt me, I could return the favor.

"She is not." He scoffed. "Don't be crazy."

Oh, *hell* no. He had a death wish. I stomped my foot, channeling Luna. "Griffin," I whined and pouted, sticking my bottom lip out as far as it would go. "You left me." I straightened, not able to keep up the charade, and patted my chest and rolled my eyes. "You're right. My bad. She totally isn't trying to manipulate you."

"Jealousy is a good look on you." He wrapped an arm around my waist and pulled me hard against his chest. "In fact, it's sexy. Maybe I should rile you up more often."

The *tug* strengthened to where it felt like two magnets were pulling toward each other.

My body warmed in ways it never had before, and I didn't even try to move away.

"You *are* attracted to me too." He dipped his head, and the world around us disappeared, the connection between us too strong to be ignored. His lips aimed for mine as my rationale left me. I couldn't remember why this was a bad idea.

The back door jingled and opened. "Dove?" Killian called.

CHAPTER TEN

I shoved Griffin away and jerked back as Killian stepped onto the back porch. He paused and rubbed his chin as he took us in.

"Are you two trying to wake up the neighborhood?" he asked.

"No." I'd been aware we were getting loud, but I hadn't realized the extent.

Griffin yanked at his shirt and glared at me. "Why the hell did you shove me?"

"Because you were all up in my face." And I'd loved every second of it. I didn't even want to consider what would've happened if Killian hadn't come outside. Griffin's lips had been only a breath away from mine, and I hadn't had the fight in me to pull away.

I couldn't be alone with him. Hell, I shouldn't be around him at all, but definitely not alone.

"You weren't complaining a few seconds ago." Griffin smirked.

"What the hell does that mean?" Killian tensed and ran down the stairs, joining us in the backyard.

My body felt like it was on fire, and not the kind I'd felt moments ago. This was the kind that made me want to cover my face in shame. I'd almost broken a promise to the one person I could rely on. I had to figure out a way to salvage this. "He and I scuffled." That wasn't a lie.

"Scuffled?" Killian parroted, and his forehead etched with confusion.

"He didn't think I could kick his ass." I avoided Griffin's gaze, not wanting to see his expression. "So, I had to prove to him that I can handle myself."

"Dude, I could've told you that." Killian pointed at his face. "She broke my nose yesterday."

"Whatever," Griffin grumbled. "But it's her fault we're fighting. I was out here making sure the bear shifter wasn't around, and she came out all by herself. You'd think you wouldn't let your girlfriend come out at night alone."

"He's not my father, so I don't need his permission." God, I wanted to smack Griffin. I glared at him. "So why don't you go to Hell?"

Well, I escalated that quickly, but I couldn't control my emotions around him. This was going to be a problem.

"Oh, it's clear that he's not your father." Griffin laughed crazily. "You don't have to tell me that, but if he cares so damn much about you, then he needs to not let you go outside in the middle of the night by yourself. You could get captured or worse."

"Do we need to go over this again?" My body shook with so much anger. "I can take care of myself."

Killian touched my shoulder, and Griffin growled.

"Dude." Killian lifted his hand off me. "Are you okay?"

"I'm fine." Griffin straightened his shoulders and puffed out his chest. "More than fine. Great." The awful smell of a lie hit our noses.

"Yeah, right. If that's the case, then why are the two of you out here, yelling at each other?" Killian glanced at me before fixating on his friend again. "I mean, you say she shouldn't be outside, but if anyone was in the vicinity, they'd come check out the noise, and both of you could be in trouble."

Dammit, he was right. "Part of his concern is that the bear shifter escaped before they could get him to the jail."

"What?" Killian's mouth dropped. "How is that possible?"

Griffin's shoulders deflated, and he looked like the confused person I'd felt like earlier. He rubbed a hand down his face. "Apparently, Harold didn't follow standard police protocol, and the guy attacked him and got away." Griffin started the story from scratch, filling Killian in on everything he'd already told me.

"Why didn't you tell us this earlier?" Killian frowned. "He could try again."

"That's why I'm out here." Griffin glanced over his shoulder at the woods. "I wanted to make sure that no one was lurking around."

"We don't even know if he was targeting me." If the bear was one of the men who'd killed my pack, he would've known I was skilled and strong. He would've had backup, especially since it wasn't a new moon. I figured this had to be someone different, which made things even more complicated. "I could've been the closest wolf."

"She's right." Killian wrapped an arm around my waist as he watched Griffin. "The group that's unhappy are attacking wolves in general. Any of us could be next."

"I don't understand what's going on." I'd gleaned a lot earlier, but there were still crucial pieces of the puzzle missing. "I get that wolves are being attacked because you all opened the city back up, but I still don't understand—why only wolves?"

"Right before Dad died, he headed the initiative to open the borders, much to the chagrin of one of the angel council members and all three witch representatives. The vote was cast, and Dad got the majority by only one vote. Even though he died, there was no stopping the decision." Griffin winced with pain. "The alpha power transferred to me upon his death. At times, feeling everyone gets to be too much. That's why things have fallen apart since then."

"Any transition has road bumps." Killian tried to reassure him. "We've talked about this."

"And I told you that I'm not ready to be alpha. I could never be the kind of leader Dad was." Griffin rubbed his hands together. "The only reason I haven't handed the reins over to Dick permanently is all the turmoil going on. Once things are settled, I'll figure out my next steps."

Everyone fell silent, and after a prolonged moment, I forced a yawn. I'd come out here to find comfort and refuge, but all I'd gotten was drama and angst. "I'm exhausted. I'm going to bed."

"Shouldn't you go home?" Griffin rasped.

"Dude," Killian said, "she's staying with me for a while."

He raised both hands. "I was thinking if the bear attacked her because she was with us, staying away would be the best idea."

"I'm done having the same conversation with you over and over." I glared at him. "I've already kicked your ass, so drop it." I marched up the steps to the back porch and entered the house, leaving the two idiots outside.

When the door closed, I leaned against the wall, trying to find some sort of calm.

"Why are you being such an asshole to her?" Killian

growled, and I startled, realizing I was in the perfect place to eavesdrop. I held my breath, trying to make sure I heard everything. Killian continued, "Is it because I got her first?"

"What?" Griffin said, sounding surprised. "No."

"Then what the hell is it?" Killian pushed harder.

My breath caught as I eagerly awaited his answer. I didn't know why, but his answer was so damn important to me.

"Man, I don't know." Griffin sighed. "She gets under my skin, and I have no clue why."

"Could it be because she shut you down when you tried hitting on her?" Killian asked.

"Maybe. I don't know, man." Griffin sounded conflicted. "I mean, don't get me wrong. I'm thrilled she shut me down since she has you, and I would've never hit on her if I'd known she was the girl you told me about last night. I think it's partly because she appeared out of nowhere, and now she's sleeping at your house. How much do you even know about her?"

I turned toward the door, ready to go back outside to interrupt their conversation. I didn't need Griffin learning about everything. He'd use it to his advantage. My hand reached the doorknob when Killian said, "Look, I appreciate you looking out for me. And there is a reason it happened so quickly. But it's not my place to tell you. Cut her some slack."

My hand fell to my side as my heart broke all over again. Killian had kept his word, but my gut said Griffin would start digging harder. I had to make sure I didn't let anything slip.

After all, my life depended on it.

A KNOCK on the door slammed me back to the present. I sat upright in the bed and glanced around, expecting someone to pop out from under the bed or out of the closet.

"Dove?" Killian said and knocked again.

"Come in." I pulled the covers over me for some dumb-ass reason. I had on a pair of pajama bottoms and a shirt. In fact, they were the same ones I'd worn outside during the whole weird conversation with Griffin. If I could even call it a conversation. It was more like rage, sexual tension, and me fighting off the urge to lick his entire body.

What the hell? Why was I thinking about licking him? That was wrong on all kinds of levels.

The door opened, and Killian sauntered in. He paused and glanced around the room, and I wondered if he was thinking about me living among his sister's things.

"Do you want me to come out instead?" I hadn't even thought about him not wanting to walk in here. He usually did stay in the hallway or in the living room.

"No, it's fine." He smiled sadly. "It's kind of nice to have you in her room. It brings a little bit of happiness to the space, the same way it felt when she was alive. Although she'd cry knowing that you didn't approve of her wardrobe. She and Mom loved going shopping together." He chuckled.

"Her clothes are great, just not my style. Did I over-sleep?" If he was anything like me, he didn't want to continue that line of conversation. I glanced at the clock on the side table and read that it was seven in the morning.

"Nope, but we need to run and get your fake ID." He chuckled. "Carter will lose his shit if you show up without it again, so let's not stir the beast within."

I'd forgotten all about that. "Yeah, sounds great." Having an ID would mean I could open a checking account and other things. "I'll get dressed now."

Within thirty minutes, we were pulling into the break-fast diner where I'd seen the auburn-bearded man yester-day. I tried to calm my racing heart, but there wasn't much I could do about it. In the past, when I got nervous, I'd used my pack link to help calm me down, but I didn't have that now. Of course, that only made me panic even more.

"What's wrong?" Killian asked as he pulled into a metered spot alongside the road. "Your heart is pounding so hard I can hear it over the music. I don't think it could race any faster without you having a heart attack."

Yeah, tell me about it. "It's nothing," I said with a cracked voice as the smell of rotting eggs filled the car.

"No, seriously." He gagged at the smell. "What's wrong, and please don't lie. I haven't eaten, so it won't take much to make my stomach queasy."

"Remember when I freaked out yesterday?" I gestured to the red light we'd been stopped at.

He nodded.

"Well, that's the diner those guys came out of." I was being ridiculous, but I couldn't hold it in. Flashes of only two days ago replayed in my head, and the attack in the bar hadn't helped. I didn't want to go in there. I almost felt frozen in place.

"I'll be right there with you." Killian took my hand and gently pulled me so I faced him. "I won't leave your side."

He meant for that to be comforting, but he couldn't make that kind of promise. I hated feeling so weak and pathetic, but my wolf pawed against my head.

"Hey." He cupped my cheek. "Breathe."

But I couldn't even when I tried. I had to get away and connect with my wolf. It was the only way to become calm. "I've gotta go. I'm sorry." I pulled away from Killian and threw open the door. "I have to get away. Please don't follow me. I need a moment by myself. Just...get my ID please. I'll meet you back here in twenty."

"Dammit, Dove." Killian hissed as I slammed the door.

I'd apologize later, but the edges of my vision were starting to darken. I ran as fast as I could in the direction we'd come from toward the nearest woods. Maybe I'd regret it if I got caught, but I was about to lose myself.

My head swam as I pushed my legs to keep moving across the last road before the tree line. My eyes locked on my end destination.

A loud honk hit my ears, followed by squealing tires and the stench of burning rubber. I froze and faced the car as an older man stuck his head out and asked, "Are you okay, miss?"

I didn't have the luxury of responding, or I'd pass out before I could shift. Instead, I burst back into a run and continued on, thanking the gods that I hadn't gotten hit.

"Miss!" the guy yelled after me.

As soon as I'd run far enough into the woods to be out of sight from the road, I yanked my shirt from my body while kicking off my shoes and then pulled off the rest. I threw the clothes in one heaping pile so I could find them again easily. Then I called for my wolf.

She sprang forward with no hesitation, and I shifted faster than I ever had before. When I hit the ground on all fours, I ran deeper into the woods, needing to keep my wolf form hidden. I sniffed the air, making sure no one was close by.

Nothing smelled of other shifters or supernaturals.

Animals rustled around the woods, making my restlessness ease some. In this form, I could breathe, but the paranoia was still too damn close for comfort. I'd been packless for only a little over two days, and it was already beginning to take its toll.

I'd heard stories about how some wolves could go months before getting to this point, so why was I so different? The answer rang in my head—because I was an alpha with no pack to lead. It probably would have helped if I'd stayed under the moon longer last night, but with Griffin there, it hadn't been possible.

A rabbit jumped out from behind a tree, landing in my path, and my wolf grew excited. She wanted to be the predator and let our natural instincts take over. To lose our mind in the moment.

I chased the rabbit, the animal hopping off, running for its life. I didn't plan on eating it, just enjoyed the chase as nature intended.

The little sucker hopped faster than I expected, and my legs burned from the exercise. The paranoia receded as I lost myself in the task.

Minutes later, wings flapped, breaking my concentration. I skidded to a stop as I tried to figure out where the noise was coming from. I was used to worrying about creatures on the ground, not in the sky.

The thunder of large wings grew louder, and a familiar rose scent hit my nose. I looked up in time to see Rosemary descend between two trees, beautiful dark-feathered wings stretched out behind her back.

I wasn't used to looking out for angels, seeing as I'd never met one before her. I had to get out of here. I spun and took off in the direction of my clothes. I should've paid more attention to staying hidden, but I'd been trying to get myself under control before being stuck in the coffee shop for hours.

Hoping to lose her, I ran back toward the road. But

suddenly, something was standing right in my path. I skidded to a halt, weighing my options.

"Well, isn't this quite interesting," Rosemary said as she crossed her arms. "I thought I smelled a strange wolf below."

No.

No one could know who I was.

CHAPTER ELEVEN

I f I could have beaten myself up for my carelessness, I
would have. I *knew* not to shift, but I'd been losing my
damn mind and had needed an outlet. By letting my wolf
take control, I hadn't stayed focused on my surroundings as
I should have. I was having fun chasing down a flipping
rabbit.

Rosemary's charcoal wings spread out, causing her hair
to blow around her face. She was somehow even more
breathtaking in this form, and I was almost thankful I was in
animal form, or I'd have been gawking.

This was the first time I'd seen an angel with wings, and
now her rose scent made sense. But I had no clue how her
gray sweater wasn't torn to threads.

Thankfully, I couldn't speak to her in wolf form, so it
wasn't like I'd be able to answer any of the questions that
had to be churning in her mind. I could only hope that she
didn't know who I was. Granted, whether Rosemary knew
it was me or not, the news of a silver wolf being seen
running around near town would cause a lot of excitement
and would inevitably get back to the people hunting me.

"What is a silver wolf doing here? I thought they were extinct." She arched an eyebrow as she examined my body. "You need to shift back into human form before someone else sees you.'"

Out of every possible scenario, I did not see that one coming. I figured she'd be eager to expose my existence.

"That means you better move your ass now." She waved a hand for added emphasis. "More people run in this section of the woods, so the longer you stay like this, the more likely others will see you."

She was right. These woods were near downtown and close to campus. My dad had been lecturing me about not thinking like a leader, and this proved he was right. Making dumb mistakes like this solidified that I needed him here with me. Not dead. I wasn't anywhere near ready to lead or even survive on my own without a pack.

Hysteria inched closer to the surface, and I took a deep breath, attempting to keep the negative emotions at bay. I couldn't afford to do another stupid thing.

Not wanting to get close to Rosemary, I nodded and took off, giving her a wide berth. I'd never been around angels before, but I had a feeling they would have an excellent sense of smell like most supernaturals, so the farther I stayed away, the less likely she'd figure out who I was.

Not altering my plan, I rushed back in the direction of my clothes. However, this time, I kept my eyes and ears peeled for sounds coming from any angle. Luckily, all I heard were the animals that naturally lived in the woods.

As I got closer to the edge of the woods near downtown, I slowed to a trot. When I reached my clothes, I scanned the area one more time before shifting back to my human form and getting dressed. I ran a hand through my hair, making sure there weren't any branches or grass stuck in it. I yanked my black top down over my jeans and forced my legs to propel me forward.

I needed to get out of here before Rosemary found me again. I didn't need to help her connect the dots.

This time, instead of almost getting hit, I checked both ways before crossing the street. If that car hadn't been able to stop earlier, I could've died.

What scared me was that dying didn't sound horrible.

If Zoe could hear what I was thinking now, she'd smack the hell out of me. But depression was a bitch, and I was at her mercy.

I got back to the diner as Killian exited. His eyes immediately found mine, and he hurried to me.

"I've been worried sick," he said when he caught up to me. "You freaked out on me."

That pretty much nailed my actions dead on. "Yeah, I'm sorry. The past few days kind of caught up to me, including not being part of a pack any longer. Being a rogue is beginning to take its toll."

"Shit." He ran a hand through his hair and shook his head. "I hadn't even thought about you being rogue. Maybe you can join my pack. Not that I want to be your alpha, but it's a good pack, and you have fighting skills."

"My problems aren't your responsibility." He'd already done so much by giving me a place to stay, finding me a job, getting me a fake ID, and being a friend when I didn't have anyone. He was taking all of this on like my problems were his too. "And, thank you. Let me think on that." The answer was no, but I didn't want to hurt his feelings.

"No, they aren't," he agreed and shrugged. "But I'm invested, and there's no getting rid of me. After all, you're my old hag."

A laugh slipped out, surprising me. I glanced around

and lowered my voice so no one but Killian could hear me. "Old hag? Wow. No wonder you had to con me into playing this role."

"Con." He gasped and placed a hand on his chest. "That's hurtful."

"But calling me an old hag isn't?" I pushed his arm while smiling. "You turd."

"You keep calling me names, but look what I got for you." He pulled an ID out of his pocket and held it out of my reach. "Now tell me how much you love me, or you won't be getting this."

Enjoying the lighthearted moment, I sprang into action and elbowed him in the stomach, causing him to lean forward while trying to block me. I spun out, grabbing the ID as I moved. I looked at the picture, which was the one Killian had taken that first night on his phone, and read the name.

Dove Davis.

I tapped my finger on the ID and grimaced. "Dove *Davis?*"

"Yup." Killian nodded and waggled his brows. "Double Ds, right there."

The sexual innuendo rang clear. "That's why you picked Davis?"

"Think of it as an inside joke." His smile was full of pride. "I mean, it's not like you have to pull that out whenever you meet someone."

"Even if I did, I'm pretty sure most wouldn't think about boobs." At least, I hoped not.

"Come on, let's go." He took my hand and led me to the truck. "Before you're late and Carter shits a brick."

"Wow, your eloquence is on point today." I stuck out my tongue, trying to keep the conversation lighthearted.

When we got settled in the car, Killian pulled out of the parking spot and glanced at me. "You do realize that the longer you stay rogue, the more your mind will slip."

"I know, but what am I supposed to do?" I stared at my hands. "It's not like finding a pack that works for me is a simple thing to do. I'm an alpha." I wouldn't be able to submit to another alpha. Dad was the alpha when I was born, and he was also my parent, so accepting his authority over me hadn't been an issue. But I was born to lead, which made this whole situation complicated. I wouldn't be able to join a pack unless I could be the alpha. My wolf wouldn't let me, and there wasn't going to be a current alpha who would stand down... especially for a girl. Male alphas tended to frown upon women in leadership roles, although that made me even more determined to prove myself.

I got that Killian didn't want to be an alpha—at least, not yet—but I didn't want to take over his pack. That wouldn't feel right. I could tell he was meant to lead.

"Why am I not surprised by that? That does make things way more complicated. Maybe we should try running together," he suggested.

"No!" I said quickly.

His face fell, and his hands fidgeted on the steering wheel.

Great, I'd hurt his feelings. I hadn't meant to. Rosemary already knew the truth; maybe I should let him in too. "There's another reason I can't run with you or join your pack."

"And what's that?" His forehead lined with confusion. He was making it abundantly clear that he wouldn't be dropping it, and in fairness, with the way he was helping me, he had a right to know. "Can you not shift or something?"

120 JEN L. GREY

"You have to swear that if I tell you this, it stays between us. *No one* else can know. Not Griffin. Nobody." The last thing I needed was Griffin or Luna finding out unless they *had* to be let in on my secret later. Or if Rosemary figured out who I was and told people.

"If I haven't proven my trustworthiness by now, I'm not sure what else I can do." Killian scowled.

Fair enough, but I'd known him for only two days. It was kind of insane to think about revealing what I was to anyone after living my entire life in secret, but all I got was good vibes from him. I'd have to go with my gut.

"Have you heard of silver wolves?" Maybe he could figure it out on his own instead of me having to say the actual words.

"The race of wolves that once served as the protectors of Shadow City and were connected to the moon?" He nodded. "Atticus raised Griffin on stories about them. They sounded badass. It's too bad that they died off. I heard that they were powerful."

"Well, they all did die off—two days ago. Except for one, who managed to escape." I said the words quietly, bracing for his reaction.

He blinked a few times, staring straight ahead as the words settled over him. He inhaled. "You're a *silver wolf?*" He turned to face me. "How the hell is that possible? Your race left the city over one thousand years ago and vanished."

There had to be a piece of the story missing. "Atticus knew my dad, who was the alpha of our pack. My dad even visited the city at least once because Atticus wanted us to come back."

"Why did your ancestors leave?" He rolled his shoulders. "Did whoever attacked you know what your pack was?"

"All I know is that we left because things were taking a turn, and our race was being used for corrupt things." Dad never got into specifics. He'd said he'd tell me more when the time came for me to lead the pack. But that wasn't relevant now. "And the people who killed my pack knew. They attacked on the new moon when we're at our weakest and more in line with the strength of a normal wolf shifter. What I can figure is that they wanted to capture me alive so they could take me to someone to make babies with him."

"Why would anyone want to be forced into a mate bond?" He lifted a hand. "Not that you aren't gorgeous. I'd be all up on you if you didn't remind me of my sister."

For once, I was speechless. A car blew a horn, startling me. Both Killian and I looked out the windshield and found ourselves barreling down the wrong lane right toward a huge SUV.

"Fuck!" Killian yelled as he jerked the steering wheel hard to the right.

My breath caught as my head snapped sideways. I closed my eyes, bracing for impact, and forced my body to relax, remembering one of the training exercises Dad made us do regularly. When your body was relaxed, you didn't get as injured as if you tensed up. That was one reason that drunk drivers so often walked away from an accident without injury.

After a few seconds, nothing happened, and I opened my eyes to find Killian wiping his forehead then clenching the wheel extra hard.

He glanced at me. "Are you hurt?"

"Eyes on the road." I snapped, not wanting to experience that again. "If you can't stay focused, we can chat later."

"I'm fine now." He patted his chest. "I knew you had secrets, but I would've never guessed that."

No one would. "To answer your question, any child I bear will be a full-blooded silver wolf."

"How is that possible?" He grimaced. "I mean, wouldn't that be only if you mated with another silver wolf?"

"Let me repeat." I chuckled. "Any child I bear will be one hundred percent silver wolf. It has to do with our connection to the moon."

"How could you know that unless..." He trailed off. "Did your pack mate with normal wolves? Have you *not* been hidden all this time? Why haven't any of us heard you exist?"

He was asking a lot of good questions that I'd never thought about before. "Yes, sometimes, although we did stay hidden as much as possible. We integrated into society to find our fated mates—no one outside our pack was allowed to be brought home unless they were a pack member's fated mate. Because of that connection and the need to keep growing our pack, those were the exceptions. However, we'd go to the grocery store and school like any other wolf would. We just didn't shift with outside wolves or invite them to our homes. We kept a safe distance from them."

"That's insane." Killian turned the truck toward the entrance of Shadow Ridge University. "So whoever this person is wants you so he can father silver wolves. This is so much worse than I expected."

And that was when it hit me. Now that he knew my entire story, he might not want me around. I couldn't blame him, with the danger hanging over me. "I get it if you want me to leave."

"Of course I don't." He reached over and patted my arm. "You're only the second person I've truly connected with since my own family died. And honestly, the reason I live in the Ridge is because my pack became the protectors once the silver wolves left. Maybe with you by my side, I could become the type of alpha my pack needs and the two of us can work together."

"Really?" I'd never thought Shadow City would replace us. "And you do miss being close with your pack."

"Yeah, so I think it's cool that history has kind of come full circle." He rolled down his window and scanned his card. "And I do, but it's so hard to look at my pack members, knowing I failed not only them but my family. In a way, this has to be destiny."

My heart fractured. "My parents and pack being slaugh-tered was *destiny*?"

"Dammit. I didn't mean it like that." He cleared his throat as he rolled his window back up. "Let's talk about this more later."

"Okay, but there's something else you need to know." I stared at the building in front of us. "When I kind of lost it earlier, I ran into the nearest woods and shifted."

"While I was getting your ID?" he asked, his words care-ful, not conveying any sort of emotion.

"Yes, and someone saw me." If he got upset with me, he'd have the right. Since he was providing shelter for me, when I did anything stupid, it could fall back on him.

His jaw clenched. "Griffin?"

"*What?*" Out of all of the people he might guess, I hadn't expected that one. "No, not him."

"Thank God." His shoulders relaxed. "Then who?"

"Rosemary." The next words left my mouth faster than ever before. "But she didn't see me in human form, so maybe she won't know it was me."

"I take it back." He tensed. "I would rather it have been

Griffin after all. If Rosemary figures it out, that's going to be an even bigger problem."

"Why?" If she was a bigger threat, then there was no telling what we could be walking into on campus.

CHAPTER TWELVE

The car clock showed two minutes 'til nine. I hated to cut this conversation short, however, I needed the job. I hoped that Rosemary wouldn't ruin it for me, but I couldn't hide like a coward. She seemed like she might not want others to know about me, so I'd hold on to that until she proved otherwise. "We've got to hurry or I'm going to be late."

"Are you sure it's smart going in there?" Killian cracked his knuckles. "Rosemary isn't known for being patient. And if she figures it out, she'll alert her mom, Yelahiah, who happens to be a council member of Shadow City."

Which meant every leader in the city would find out about me. Dammit. "If I don't show up, then it might confirm what she suspects. And if you're right and she doesn't keep her mouth shut, then I'm going to look guilty for not coming to work." If she did start talking, I needed to know as fast as possible. The longer she ran her mouth and I didn't know, the more at risk I'd be from whomever was hunting me.

My stomach churned.

Being a rogue wolf was already taking its toll, even with Killian by my side. I couldn't imagine what it'd be like all on my own with not even a friend. Relationships were so damn important to wolves.

"Fine, but one funny look, and we're out of there." He looked at me sternly. "You have to at least promise me that."

I was damn lucky to have found him. "Got it."

"Promise?" he pushed.

He already knew my stubborn ass too well. "Yes, promise."

He must have seen what he was looking for because he opened his door and climbed out. Normally he'd run over and open mine, but I had one minute to get inside. I got out and joined him behind the truck. Not missing a beat, the two of us rushed into the building and made our way to the coffee shop.

When we approached the shop, the line was already out the door and into the hallway. I shouldn't have been surprised—most of the people in line looked like they could fall asleep standing right there.

I sprinted to the counter where Carter stood grumpily in front of the cash register as one lanky crow shifter made drinks.

Carter sniffed as I got closer, and he let out a huge sigh, "It's about time you got here."

"Oh, come on." Killian chuckled as he caught up to me. "She's one minute late. I'm pretty sure that line didn't miraculously appear during the last minute."

"No, but Deissy called out sick again." Carter frowned. "I told her don't bother coming in ever again."

"You pulled the plug on her?" Killian sounded mildly impressed. "What made you finally do it?"

"Because you found someone to replace her." Carter held up a finger to the customer standing in front. "Please hold on one second." He turned to me. "But I need that ID now. I got screamed at by HR for letting you work yesterday."

The fact that he planned to keep me on helped with some of my turmoil. At least, I had something I could kind of call my own.

"Oh, here." Thank God Killian had come through for me. I handed Carter my ID and slipped on an apron. "Anything else?" At least, he was acting normal, not that he would've heard the latest gossip with the shop insanely busy.

"Yes." Carter hissed at the cash register like it was the demon he'd said lived in it. "Work that damn thing."

I grinned as I reached the register. Carter already seemed to rely on me, which thrilled me.

"When does she get off?" Killian asked.

"Come get her after the noon rush, but I'll want her here earlier tomorrow morning," Carter answered.

Killian blew me a kiss as he walked out the door, and then I focused on my task at hand.

FOR THE FIRST HOUR, my heart picked up its pace every time someone entered the shop. Each time, I expected to see the gorgeous dark angel who'd found me in the woods this morning. But she never came. Maybe she had no clue who I was after all. Or maybe she didn't care.

Angels were supernatural and could fly, and they had super strength and other magical abilities, but their nose wasn't as sensitive as a wolf's or a bear's.

Maybe I was safe after all. Maybe I hadn't needed to reveal my secret to Killian. In fear, I'd rushed to tell him, not wanting him to hear it from anyone else. Knowing what I was put him in so much danger, but I couldn't rewind and change the past.

But boy, I sure wished I could. That ability would have been so nice to have. My pack would still be alive, and I'd be with Dad, training for the day I took over the pack.

Someone cleared his throat, and I looked up to see a man who looked a few years older than me. "Are you okay, miss?" His sharp angular face brought out soft blue eyes that were full of concern. He pulled his wallet from his khaki pants and scratched his golden-brown hair. He had a regal presence to him, and he smelled like maple syrup, which screamed vampire.

"Yes, sorry." I forced a small laugh that sounded like a cough. "I spaced for a minute."

"Spaced?" His face lined with confusion.

"I was daydreaming." God, that sounded horrible. "But don't worry, it wasn't about you." *Come on, Sterlyn. Get your shit together.*

The vampire laughed and handed me his credit card. "I asked for a black coffee."

"Of course." I inhaled deeply, forcing my body to relax. I took his card and swiped it and then hurried off to fill a cup.

I didn't even know vampires drank coffee. Obviously, they did, or he wouldn't be here, asking for it. Generally, the vampires we had encountered were focused on one thing— blood. We had to protect the nearby town several times because of vampire outbreaks. When a vampire lost their humanity, they turned deadly, draining humans to death, and the sun began to harm them. Each kill weakened their soul to the point where even the moonlight could hurt them.

As the cup filled, a rose scent hit my nose, and the sense of peace I'd found evaporated like the feeling had been a figment of my imagination.

My hands shook as I put the lid on the coffee. Freaking out would only make the situation worse. I turned, plastering a fake smile securely on my face, and handed the attractive man his drink. "Do you need anything else?"

"No, thank you." He winked and headed out the door, walking up to what had to be shifter. I kept my gaze on him, not wanting to meet her gaze.

Rosemary *tsk*ed as she propped her hip against the counter. "I'm thinking Killian wouldn't approve of you checking out Alex like that."

"Alex?" What was she talking about? I'd expected her to throw her accusations at me. Not talk to me like nothing had happened.

"The vampire prince who got coffee and left. The one you watched walk out the door like he was the only thing you could focus on?" She tapped a finger against her lip and then wagged it at me. "That's right. You aren't from Shadow City or Shadow Ridge. Where exactly did you come from again?"

"A place not too far from here." The emotion wafting off her was confusion. Like she was trying to figure out something. I had to be very careful how I played this.

"How far?" She leaned closer to me. "Like an hour or several?"

Unfortunately, there was no lying now, so I was stuck in this conversation. "About twenty miles. Do you want something to drink?" Giving her an approximate mileage wasn't the best idea, but it would be hard for her to pinpoint. And if she was sniffing out silver wolves, no one would say anything. The only ones who knew, outside of me, Killian, and a bunch of murderers, were dead.

"Yeah." She looked around the register at Carter. "How about a mocha with four extra shots of espresso?"

"On it." He nodded like that request wasn't odd.

I almost wanted to say something about her heart not liking it, but I figured the joke would fall flat, and with her being one of the strongest supernaturals around, there wasn't much that would hurt her heart, to begin with. I rang up her order and prayed she wouldn't continue her investigation.

"Funny thing happened this morning," she whispered. "I flew over the woods and caught some shifter chasing a rabbit."

Yup, she thought it was me, but the confusion rolling off her calmed me. She was watching my reaction, trying to glean something from me.

"Depending on the shifter, that would make sense." I looked at her and smiled. She wanted me to slip up and say wolf to confirm it was me.

The edges of her mouth tipped downward for a second before she schooled her expression into a mask of indifference.

"That'll be $6.73," I said, forcing my voice to sound even. I needed her to drop this entire conversation, but I couldn't let her realize that she was affecting me.

She rocked on her heels as she pulled some cash from her back pocket. "You know, I love your hair. Do you dye it?" Her gaze remained on me.

Luckily, I had dyed my hair once. I was so tired of having the silver hair that continually reminded kids my age I was their future leader. I had wanted to blend in, but much to my horror, the color didn't stick. My hair stayed the exact same shade it was now. "Yeah, I've dyed it."

"Interesting." She handed the money to me.

I made sure to keep my hands steady as I made change. "Is your hair natural?" Everything inside me wanted me to change the subject, which meant I couldn't.

Her eyes widened marginally. "Yes, this is my natural hair color. Angels don't normally alter their appearance. We don't even wear makeup." The superiority of her tone grated on my nerves.

"I figured fallen might think differently." I was pushing her buttons on purpose. If I made her mad, maybe she'd drop the third degree. In reality, I wasn't sure if she had fallen or been born to fallen parents.

"Well, you obviously don't know much about angels, do you?" She lifted her chin in defiance before something settled over her.

She seemed more confused now than when she came in.

"Here you go, Rosemary," Carter said as he handed her the mocha while giving me the side-eye.

I'd get a lecture about being more professional when she was gone, my second one, and I'd been on the job only two days. This Deissy girl must be horrid if he was thrilled to hire me in her stead.

"Thanks." Rosemary took the drink but didn't leave. "There's something about you, *Dove*. Maybe it's not what I thought, but that doesn't mean I won't figure it out."

A small amount of respect filled me for this beautiful girl. She was direct almost to a fault, but I appreciated knowing exactly where I stood with her. One of the unique powers silver wolves got from the moon was the ability for us to read someone's intention. Rosemary wanted to be honorable, but she hadn't quite figured that out yet.

She turned to leave, and my gaze landed where her wings had been earlier. I noticed two slits in the back of her sweater, wide enough for the wings to spring from. The material almost hid them.

Another interesting fact that I learned today—angels had special clothing.

"How many times are we going to have this conversation?" Carter groaned. "You can't antagonize the customers, especially ones tied to the council."

He continued to ramble, but my focus remained on Rosemary as she left the shop. For now, she hadn't put it together that I was the silver wolf. She suspected it, but I'd managed not to confirm it. I had to keep it that way, or Killian and I could be in a world of hurt.

THE NEXT WEEK and a half passed in a blur. Each day, I grew jumpier, between my missing pack and, disturbingly, not seeing Griffin. What bothered me most was that missing the sexy douchebag kept him constantly on my mind and on alert for him.

I hadn't seen him since the night of our almost kiss. I tried not to look for him, but I couldn't help myself. His face, his smell, his presence...being without him had left a hole inside me, making me desperate to see him again.

He didn't appear to be staying at his house, and Killian had muttered that he hadn't heard from his best friend either. The last he'd heard, Griffin was going to Shadow City to spend time with his mom and try to determine who was behind the attacks on wolves, but every time Killian called, Griffin didn't answer.

The most concerning part was that Luna had been missing in action too. I didn't want to consider what those two were up to. It made me want to puke.

"Dove?" Carter called.

I was getting used to the name. I never would've expected that, but it had become mildly comforting. Probably because Killian had given it to me.

The coffee shop was dead. I'd been working longer days, and it was now nearly two in the afternoon, and we were closing up.

"Do you mind taking the trash out?" He pointed at the garbage can.

Carter acted like I wouldn't do it without him reminding me. "I've taken it out for the past five days." I finished counting out the cash drawer, headed over to the trash, and tied up the bag. "I'll be right back."

He nodded and continued wiping down the counters. "Holler if you need anything."

I walked through the kitchen, where the two kitchen girls were cleaning up the food mess from the day, and straight out the back to the garbage bin. The rancid smell of decaying food slammed into me. Since I was new, I got to be the one to deal with this. Something about seniority, and after the first time, I understood why. No one, not even a human, would want to come out here and smell this.

Holding my breath, I hurried to the large, blue dumpster outside the back door and threw the bag inside. I spun around...and silver paint on the brick caught my eye.

No.

This couldn't be.

Why would Rosemary do this to me? My breathing

quickened. I was so upset that the awful garbage smell didn't even register any longer.

I rushed over and traced the drawing on the wall. It was of a wolf in silver paint, the combination telling. It couldn't be a coincidence. That would be too convenient at this point.

My vision grew hazy. I had to get something to clean this off or paint to spray over it. No one could see this.

CHAPTER THIRTEEN

Time was ticking, and I needed to get back inside. But I couldn't risk leaving this drawing out here where someone else might see it. This was a hidden message for me; it had to be. Most people probably wouldn't think much about it, but I didn't want to chance any sort of talk starting about a silver wolf painted on this building. The people hunting me could hear about it and come by to check it out.

I shuddered, remembering that whomever they worked for wanted me to have his babies.

A *breeder*.

The thought of what that would entail made a shiver run down my spine.

Every night, I dreamed that they found me, and I'd wake up in a cold sweat and not be able to go back to sleep. A run would make things better, but I couldn't risk it after last week in the woods.

To make matters worse, Rosemary had been feeling me out each day when she grabbed her morning coffee. Maybe this painting was how she was forcing my hand. She'd been growing frustrated with my evasiveness, so she wanted me to react and confirm it was me. She must be dedicated to getting to me to paint the wolf out here while enduring the smell, even if her nose wasn't as sensitive.

I hated to admit that her plan was effective. But I'd deal with that bitch later. I had to focus on the most immediate problem so I didn't get overwhelmed.

The trouble was I had no clue how to remove or cover up the wolf. I searched the area, trying to find something—anything—to help me fix this situation. I relaxed my arms and shoulders, trying to remove the panic from my mind. If I let the fear take hold, I wouldn't be able to figure out a solution... if there even was one.

Ignoring the putrid smell, I walked around the edge of the cement, staring into the distance, but there wasn't a damn thing that could help. All that was back here was the large blue dumpster, trash, and cement. There were a few trees not far away, but that wouldn't help me any.

Dammit.

Maybe the person had tossed the spray paint in the dumpster.

Holding my breath, I lifted the lid and stuck my head into the opening, but nothing but plastic bags of spoiled food and coffee grounds could be seen. I dropped back down to my feet and squatted, looking under the small crack of space between the bottom of the dumpster and the ground.

Small wheels on both ends of the dumpster caught my eye. I could roll it closer to the door, at least temporarily. Few people came back here, so there wasn't a *huge* risk of anyone else seeing it, but I didn't need to take the chance. The dumpster was large enough to block the painting from view.

The idea of touching that disgusting dumpster made me

gag, but my life was way more important. Besides, the paint-ing's existence put Killian at risk too. This wasn't about keeping me safe.

With renewed determination, I walked behind the dumpster and pushed it toward the wall, tapping into my wolf. At the first push, something brown drizzled from one of the crevasses and almost spilled on my shoe. I jerked my foot out of the way in the nick of time.

A glutton for punishment, I leaned over to examine the liquid more. It reminded me of the murky brown Tennessee River, which was disgusting in its own right. I pretended the liquid was coffee even though my nose screamed how wrong I was.

Footsteps sounded from inside the building toward the exterior door. I pushed harder, needing to get the dumpster over to block the painting and fast. However, even with my strength, it was slow going.

I hadn't gotten it over the wolf yet when the door opened. Thankfully, Killian's musky sandalwood scent covered up a portion of the stench.

He stepped outside and grabbed his nose. "Oh, God. Carter wasn't kidding when he told me to hold my breath."

He had a flair for the dramatic. "You can smell it in the hallway, so you should've known."

"It wasn't nearly as bad there. It's like someone magic-spelled the hallway to take down their enemies by luring them through it and then shoving them out the door." Killian shivered. "Carter said you've been out here for a while and that I should check on you. I thought he was over-reacting until now."

I understood he was trying to be cute and funny, but now wasn't the time. "I've got a problem."

"This smell—"

"No, I'm being serious." I wasn't trying to be a bitch, but I needed him to focus. "Look." I gestured to the brick.

He pinched his nose, keeping up his antics, until his gaze fell on the silver wolf on the wall. "Holy shit." He glanced around and then sighed. "That could be awful luck."

"Let's see." The more I thought about the situation, the more I realized that this was done on purpose. "I've been the only person taking the trash out the past five days I've worked. Someone painted this back here where it smells like ass. And Rosemary has been sniffing around me since she found me in the woods last week."

"You had me at them coming back here and smelling this shit on their own terms." Killian sucked in a breath and pretended to dry heave. "I have got to stop doing that."

"Will you help me?" I nodded toward the other end of the dumpster. "The only solution is to use this to cover it until I can get back and spray paint over it."

"Of course. Let's do it." He clutched the other end of the dumpster and helped me guide it to the wall. Once it was positioned over the drawing, he frowned. "Go in before Carter comes back out here. I'll run to one of the hardware stores and get some spray paint. There's one not too far from here. I'll paint over the wolf and meet you out front."

He was already doing too much. "If Rosemary finds out that you know my secret, then she could lump you in with me too. I don't want the council to be out for you."

"If she knows, then she'll assume that I know too." He placed a hand on my arm. "Especially with how a girlfriend suddenly popped up."

Ugh, I hadn't thought of that. But he was right. "Fine, I'll go in before someone else comes out here and snoops around."

"I'll be back and meet you out front." Killian removed the keys from his pocket. "Finish closing up the shop."

"Are you sure?" Leaving him to clean up my mess didn't settle well with me, but at the same time, having someone come back here and see the painting sounded worse. "Thank you."

"Of course." He kissed my cheek. "You're one of my best friends now. I'd do anything for you." He walked around the building, heading to his truck.

How I wished we felt a romantic connection to each other. He was the type of guy my dad would've been so proud that I found. He was kind, considerate, and loyal. Although, if my dad was still alive, Killian and I probably wouldn't have become friends even if the silver wolves had returned to Shadow City. We'd bonded over the loss of our families and created a connection through that.

Forcing myself to go back into the building, I rushed to the bathroom to wash my hands. As I looked in the mirror, I almost didn't recognize the girl staring back at me. My silver hair was pulled back into a bun, and my silver-purple eyes had darkened to almost steel gray. Hell, with the paleness of my skin, I could almost pass for a vampire.

My clothes were a little baggy on me, due to all the stress. Every time I tried to eat, I'd lose my appetite after a few bites. Lately, I'd been living on coffee, which amped me up even more on top of everything else. At some point, I would have to risk shifting and taking a run.

Turning away from the mirror, I cranked the paper towel dispenser and wiped down my hands and face. I tossed the paper towel into the garbage and pinched my cheeks, trying to add a little color to my skin, then left the bathroom.

The two girls in the kitchen were gone, and when I walked out front, only Carter remained.

He leaned over, trying to see behind me, and sniffed. "How'd you lose Killian? I need you to teach me that little trick."

Carter and Killian loved giving each other hell, but I could tell there was mutual respect on both sides.

"He was whining about the smell and said he needed to run to the store, so he took off." I placed a hand on my hip and forced a smile, trying to act somewhat normal. However, my mind kept seeing the artwork I'd left behind. "I'm assuming the smell is why you sent him out there in the first place."

"Maybe." He shrugged. "He did leave me drunk off my ass at a party a couple of weeks ago with this girl I can't stand wrapped all around me." He shuddered at the memory. "All the things she did to me that night I can't take back. But I was hoping he'd puke."

"You do realize he's a shifter." Granted, that smell was awful out there, but our stomachs were sturdy.

"But the pain is real." He nodded toward the door. "Let's get out of here."

As we left the building, a certain dark angel caught my eye. Rosemary was outside all alone, lying on top of a picnic table like she was sunbathing. She had a bag propped under her neck and shoulders as she read some sort of textbook.

Anger spread through me like wildfire. "I'll see you tomorrow," I said to Carter as I headed toward her.

"Uh, yeah. See ya." He sounded confused, but I didn't have time to focus on that.

Of course, she would be perched outside the coffee shop to watch my reaction. I shouldn't confront her—that was what she wanted after all—but I was done playing this cat and mouse game with her.

It ended now.

I marched directly toward her, welcoming the righteous anger. The emotion was a soothing relief to the stress, anxiety, and pain that I felt most of the time.

When I reached her, I stood so that my shadow blocked her sun.

She dropped her book and sighed. "Can I help you?" Even though she sounded put out, interest seemed to spark in her eyes.

"You had to do it, didn't you?" My wolf brushed against my mind. She'd been struggling and cooped up, which was a dangerous combination to my already fracturing self.

"Do what?" She placed her book down beside her and sat fully upright. She examined my face and tilted her head.

"Don't play innocent." I lifted my hands. "You're getting what you wanted. A reaction."

"Dove, what happened?" she asked, sounding perplexed.

"You want me to spell it out for you, don't you?" My emotions swirled inside me so much that I couldn't get a read on her. I was losing control, and I wasn't sure how to rein it in.

She chewed on her bottom lip. "Are you okay?"

"You drew a silver wolf by the dumpster, knowing I'd take out the garbage and see it," I hissed as my hands shook. "And you're asking me if I'm okay?"

"What?" She jumped to her feet and looked all around us. "I did no such thing."

"Oh?" I wasn't buying it. "You expect me to believe that after you've interrogated me at every opportunity the past week?"

"You're a wolf." She tapped my shoulder. "You'd know if I was lying."

Dammit. She was right. "But if it wasn't you—" My mind circled and landed me right back on the last new moon in my pack.

They'd found me. But how...? I'd been so careful. Hell, Killian didn't even know my real name because I was afraid he might slip.

I had to get out of here, and now. This would've been an excellent time to have a car... or wings. "Do you have any idea who could have done it, have you noticed anyone lurking around? You've been here every day."

"Not at all." Her wings sprang from her back, spreading out. "I'll go see if I can find anything out. In the meantime, lie low."

"Wait!" The last thing I needed was for even more people to know about me. "How many people are you going to tell?"

"Zero." Her forehead creased.

Clearly, I'd misunderstood her. "Zero? Is that the number of people you *won't* tell?" I couldn't hide the sarcasm that laced each word.

"Believe it or not, I don't want anyone else finding out about you either." Rosemary tapped her fingers on her leg. "There's enough going on with the wolf attacks and another civil war brewing. The last thing we need is the story of an extinct silver wolf coming back from the dead. So many will consider you a traitor; it would cause tension to escalate."

"A *traitor?*" What kind of story was she trying to spin? "We left because people were using us to commit crimes!"

"We?" Her face fell. "How many of you are there?"

"None of your business." If I gave her a number, she

would be able to tell I was lying. But I didn't want her to think she could kill me now and eliminate the problem.

She rolled her eyes. "Look, I'll come find you when I figure out all there is to know."

Yeah, I bet she would. "Why don't you try to kill me now?" Dad had told me stories about angels not being huge fans of silver wolves.

"I don't want you dead." She laughed. "You may be a pain in the ass, but I don't need Griffin and Killian as the angels' enemies. If anything, the races need to begin working together. Don't do anything stupid until we speak again."

She took off into the sky, leaving me with my thoughts, which wasn't a good thing at this point.

A howl sounded from the woods only a few yards away, making my heart stop. I spun around and found eyes glowing at me through the tree branches.

Good. Let's get this over with. I clenched my fists, ready to fight.

CHAPTER FOURTEEN

My wolf surged forward, restless and ready to fight. Between the imminent threat and not training every day, my human and animal sides were easily excitable, and not in a good way.

I stepped toward the woods, but the wolf disappeared from sight. The padding of paws grew faint as it slipped away.

Dammit. That wolf could've overheard my entire conversation with Rosemary. And I'd been none the wiser to his presence because I was too overcome by my emotions. Dad had warned me that was what happened when you didn't think with a level head. Being rogue was clearly affecting my ability to be rational.

The urge to shift almost overwhelmed me, but I pushed my wolf back and took a moment to think. I couldn't allow my animal to take control away from my human side. If I let it happen, the rogue part I was already struggling with would get even worse.

For all I knew, the wolf shifter could've been the one

who drew the painting and had been watching my next moves to confirm it was me.

Well, if that was his end goal, I sure made it easy for him.

I should've ignored Rosemary and waited for Killian in front of the building, but something inside me had snapped. Now I wished I could take it back. If that wolf was someone scouting me out for the men who'd attacked my pack, I'd placed a flashing neon light above my head that basically said, "I'm here."

Dad had to be shaking his head at me in heaven. I kept messing up. Everything he'd taught me I'd wildly abandoned.

Maybe me not being alpha of my pack was a good thing. I wasn't wise enough to lead.

Refusing to make another damn mistake, I inhaled, filling my lungs, and cautiously approached the woods. I wouldn't go far, just try to catch the wolf's scent better. At least, that way, I would recognize him when I ran into him again.

As I approached the tree line, I stopped and listened for anything that would indicate there were more shifters close by or anyone who could possibly jump me. My too-stupid-to-live moments were done from this point forward.

Nothing sounded or smelled out of the ordinary, so I pushed forward in the direction where the eyes had been. The closer I got, the stronger his scent became, but the smell was strange. The musk that confirmed it was a wolf shifter was there, but that was about it. There wasn't anything unique about it, which meant he'd used something to mask part of his scent.

Which told me everything I needed to know.

He could be part of the pack that slaughtered my family and friends.

I had to get out of here before he circled back and brought reinforcements.

Pivoting on my heel, I made my way back toward the main building, passing four vampire girls who were hanging out in the sun. The fact that they were sitting in direct sunlight meant they still had their humanity. That reassured me that they didn't kill for pleasure and were able to control their instincts. That was a requirement in order to attend school here, most likely due to the human visitors who came to hike the amazing woods.

One of them wrinkled her nose when she saw me, proving that, like angels, vampires didn't like intermingling outside their species.

Or it could be me. I did try to give off a fuck-you vibe. The more that people talked to me, the more likely I could slip up and say something that could hint at any one of my secrets.

Pretending that I didn't notice her sour expression, I pushed through the double doors and headed straight toward the hallway.

Luna's all-too-familiar voice rang in my ear from the tables in front of the cafeteria. "Aw, did Killian leave you?"

I'd gone a little over a week without seeing her, and still enough time hadn't passed. I stopped short, making my point clear that I wouldn't try to run from her. "Nope, he needed to run an errand, and then he'll be right back." I forced a sweet smile that felt foreign. The only reaction I wanted to give her was the middle finger.

"And he didn't take you with him?" Luna sashayed over, her dark sage maxi skirt flowing out around her. She tilted her head, causing her hair to fall in front of her shoulders, brushing against her cream top. "Sounds like trouble in paradise." She turned to face a girl a couple of inches shorter than me who was following right behind her. "Jessica, you may get Killian sooner rather than later after all."

The girl's forest-green eyes focused on me, and she gave me an uncomfortable smile as she twisted chestnut hair with natural light caramel tips around one finger. Her modest pale pink wrap top complemented her medium olive complexion. "I'm sure he needed something, and things are okay between them."

Wow. I hadn't expected that.

I'd expected this girl to be as hateful or even more so than Luna, but positive energy emanated from her.

"Oh, you don't need to be nice to her." Luna waved me off. "She doesn't live in the city and never will if I have anything to say about it."

I'd never disliked someone as much as Luna before in my life. Well, correction. I outright hated the people hunting me, but she was a very close second. "Killian doesn't live in the city either."

"His best friend—my future mate—" Luna said as she patted herself on the chest "—will get him into the city where he belongs. It's only a matter of time."

That was an odd thing to say, but whatever. I didn't have time to deal with her mind games. "Great, good luck with that."

"I didn't dismiss you." She walked over to me and lifted her chin. "I'm not done talking to you."

She was grating on my nerves. I'd come inside so the wolf couldn't spy on me, but I'd rather be captured than have to deal with her. However, I had to be careful, I didn't want her to follow me outside. "What?" I couldn't hide my annoyance.

"Look, I'm trying to be nice." She scoffed and crossed her arms. "I wanted to say thank you."

She was determined to tell me whatever was on her mind. However, I wouldn't give her the satisfaction of asking. "You're welcome."

"Don't you want to know why I'm thanking you?" She pouted.

Like that was going to work. "No, but I don't think that matters. Clearly, you want to tell me."

"Griffin's been spending a lot more time in Shadow City, which has been amazing for me. I was so upset when he bought that house by Killian, but now that he's avoiding staying there, I'm wrangling him faster than I'd originally planned." She ran her hands through her hair. "I'm thinking you had something to do with that."

My wolf howled in my head so damn loud that I almost whimpered. My heart felt like it was fracturing, but that made no sense. I'd seen the guy only a couple of times, and he'd been an asshole for most of it.

They were a match made in heaven. I should have been thrilled that he had a reason to stay away...but I wasn't. I'd have liked to pretend it was because Killian missed his best friend, but that wasn't the truth. I wanted Griffin around too.

A portion of my heart grew colder at the thought of him with Luna. Not wanting to risk sounding broken, I nodded and glanced at Jessica. I forced my words to be smooth. "It was nice to meet you." And I turned and headed back out the front doors.

"What a bitch," Luna huffed. "I was thanking her."

"Well, you did tell her she'd never move into Shadow City and then in the next breath said her boyfriend would," Jessica said, "I'm thinking that hit her hard."

Not wanting to hear anymore, I stepped outside and walked onto the lawn in front of the building. The vampire girls were now watching a group of bear shifters playing football with no helmets. They had their shirts off, which almost made me laugh because their chest hair was so thick you couldn't even see their nipples.

Needing to be around noise so I couldn't hear Jessica's and Luna's conversation, I sat against a tree trunk close by and watched the idiots tackle each other over and over again.

FAMILIAR FOOTSTEPS MADE their way to me, and Killian's scent tickled my nose. I glanced toward the building and found his gaze on me.

"Are you ready to go?" he asked as his eyes flicked toward the bear shifters, who were putting on a show for the girls sitting around them.

The longer I'd sat out there, the more girls had congregated. I had to admit the bear shifters were sexy in their own right, and they were eating up the attention. Even a few angels, their floral scents giving them away, were standing around near the vampires, pretending to want to watch the game.

"Yeah." I knew I sounded terse, but, I hated being around people right now. My skin was crawling. Any time one of them made eye contact with me, I felt like they knew my secrets.

I needed to get control of my emotions because being rogue was beginning to cause even more problems. My hands kept growing sweaty, and my mind became hazy more frequently. At times, I felt a phantom pack connection that made my wolf restless. But it would vanish almost as quickly as it appeared. My wolf and I both needed to feel a connection to something, and the cold void seemed to be expanding and putting a wall up between my animal and human sides. If I didn't find a pack soon, I might go insane. Even Killian's comforting presence was having less of an effect on me. But if I became part of his pack, I'd connect with all the other hundreds, which wasn't an option. And the fact that he tried to maintain distance from his pack spoke volumes. I doubted they'd accept me—an outsider—so easily.

I had no clue what the answer was, but I needed to figure out something soon.

"Well, come on," he said and reached out a hand.

The stench of spray paint attacked my nose. I almost coughed but managed to hold it together. If the wolf was watching me, I didn't want to tip him off to what Killian had done. He could figure that out on his own. Granted, he probably wouldn't care that the image was covered. He'd painted it to get a reaction from me, and I'd already fallen into the trap.

Placing my hand in Killian's, I let him pull me to my feet, and the two of us headed toward the truck. We held an amicable silence until we were pulling out of the university.

"Were you able to cover it?" I tried not to let him know how nervous I was, but he knew me too well.

He nodded. "Yeah, I was. Sorry it took so long, but I had to make sure I didn't get caught."

"No, it's fine." His words weighed on me. "You shouldn't have done it. You're putting so much at risk by housing me and being my friend."

"Stop it." He pointed at me in warning. "That's what

friends do for one another, and come on, you know I think of you as a sister."

"Because I remind you of her." Maybe he was investing too much in me because of that. "Even though we have different tastes in clothes."

"Olive wanted to fit in with Luna and Jessica." He sighed. "She dressed more like you until the last year or so before her death, but to be clear, I'm not helping you just because you remind me of her. Maybe at first, that was why, but not anymore. You've become a true friend."

I loved that he could be honest with me. I owed him the same. "I don't want anything to happen to you. There was a wolf watching me when I went off on Rosemary."

"What are you talking about?" His brows furrowed.

I filled him in on my embarrassing display.

"That doesn't change anything, other than that we need to figure out who the wolf is." He patted my arm as he said firmly, "And we're going to get through this together. We're each other's family now. That's final."

But the problem was I couldn't agree with that. If I were in his shoes, I'd have been saying that same thing. But he'd lost his family too. And because of me, his best friend hadn't been around.

Thinking back to the night before Griffin disappeared felt like a punch to the gut. One second, we were at each other's throats, and the next second, I wanted to rip his clothes off and do things I'd never done with anyone else. I still had whiplash from my emotions that night.

The worst part was that not seeing him was driving me crazy. And to know he'd been spending time with Luna was like mixing Pop Rocks candy and Coke. I was about to explode, or implode, and I had no fucking clue why.

I decided to change the subject from something I didn't

want to talk about to something he didn't want to. It would make him shut down, at least for a little while, and I could use the reprieve. "Jessica doesn't seem all that bad." I lifted a brow at him. "In fact, she's quite breathtaking."

"How'd you meet her?" Killian pursed his lips as he glanced at me.

"Well, it involved Luna, which was very unpleasant." On so many levels. "Jessica was with her. She seems sweet."

"Jessica isn't the problem." He tapped his fingers on the steering wheel. "It's more of who her best friend is. Although honestly, what does it say about her that she chooses to be close friends with Luna?" He shuddered.

He did have a point. "They're from Griffin's pack, right?"

"Yes, and their fathers are close. They grew up together, but still. Also, my parents were fated mates, and I want to find my own. I don't want to settle for something other than that. A chosen mate is out of the cards for me. Why try to build a relationship with someone fate knows isn't for you? Why waste time in a relationship with someone when I know how it'll end?"

And he had a good point there too. If he knew what he wanted, then pushing him to do otherwise would only result in heartache.

Either way, with my secret coming out and the wolf now watching me, I knew exactly what I had to do to protect Killian and myself.

THE MOON SHONE through the window, alerting me that it was around midnight. I'd been lying in bed for hours, needing rest, but sleep wouldn't come. Each time I closed my eyes, images of my dead pack jumped vividly through my mind, but surprisingly, that wasn't the worst part. The worst part was Killian lying lifeless with them as well.

I got up and paced back and forth at the edge of the bed, trying to find some sense of calm, but it was futile.

My wolf howled in my mind, wanting to seize control, desperate to get out, and Killian's lifeless face was in every shadow of the room. Something *tugged* inside me, making my wits scatter, the sensation adding to my sense of losing control.

Terror took hold of me, and I couldn't regain my calm. My wolf surged forward, bucking against my hold.

Staying here wasn't an option any longer, but leaving would break my heart. I'd promised Killian we were in this together. However, if I didn't do something, I wasn't sure how much longer I could hold my wolf at bay.

On the nightstand sat some plain white stationary and a pen. I grabbed it quickly and wrote a note.

Killian,

Earlier when you said I was your family, I know I didn't say anything in response. But I want you to know I feel the same way about you. You've been the one bright spot since that horrible day you found me in the river.

I planned on staying like I promised, but I realized tonight that I can't put you at risk. It would be selfish of me to stay and to risk the amazing future you deserve.

I'm sorry this is how I'm saying goodbye, but I'm not strong enough to say it to your face. You've become my home, and I love you.

Your sister always,

Dove

I placed the note on my pillow, and a sob formed at the back of my throat. I swallowed it down as I opened the window, making sure not to make any noise. The bag I'd packed earlier lay on the floor with a few changes of clothes, ID, and some cash. Of course, my trusty knife was strapped to my ankle.

After grabbing the bag and tossing it through, I slipped out the window and landed on both feet. Forcing myself to stay calm, I scanned the area.

Everything looked clear.

Sighing, I picked up the bag and slung it over one shoulder. My plan was simple. Get to the river and use it to find another city or town. I'd rent a car and get as far away from here as possible. Staying near my old neighborhood must have made it easier for them to find me.

As I jogged toward the back of the house, the back porch light at Griffin's house turned on, and the back door opened.

The *tug* was so hard I nearly fell to my knees. I stopped in my tracks as emotions I didn't understand surged through me—a mixture of desire, need, and desperation.

"Dove, what the hell are you doing?" Griffin growled. "That bear shifter could be out here. Get your ass back inside."

CHAPTER FIFTEEN

My traitorous legs moved in his direction. Out of all the scenarios I'd imagined, Griffin being home wasn't one of them. He'd been gone for weeks, and all of a sudden, he reappeared tonight? *Figures. That's my luck lately.*

At least, he couldn't fight worth a damn, and the moon was already charging me. I'd kick his ass to get away if it came to that.

Not bothering to acknowledge his existence, I pressed forward, despite everything inside of me screaming to run to him and kiss his sexy mouth and touch his hard, muscular chest.

My weird attraction to him took my breath away. The time we'd spent apart from each other had only made this irrational desire even stronger. And those emotions I felt for him on top of the chaos already swirling inside made my throat dry as tears burned my eyes.

I didn't want to leave him either.

Stupid douchebag, always showing up at the worst times. Fate had a way of torturing me.

"Dove," he said, and it sounded like a warning. His feet hit the ground, coming after me. "Do not ignore me."

He moved faster than I expected him to, as if he was equally eager to get to me. But that had to be because he wanted to torment me or insult me further. My stupid legs didn't move any faster, almost as if they wanted him to catch up to me. Soon he grabbed my arm, forcing me to turn toward him.

I went to punch him but stopped short as his hazel eyes distracted me. They glowed, his wolf bleeding through and making him look even sexier. It took every ounce of my strength to keep myself from jumping into his arms.

"Does Killian know you're out here by yourself in the middle of the night?" His words held such concern. "I have a feeling he doesn't." He pushed the bag off my shoulder.

"He's not my dad—" That one word combined with Griffin's touch released the sob I'd held back, and the tears fell freely down my cheeks.

The sorrow of the past two weeks settled hard inside my chest. I hadn't truly broken down; I'd tried to focus on staying alive. But as of tonight, I'd genuinely lost everyone I cared about, one way or another. I couldn't even say *dad* without breaking down.

"Hey," Griffin said softly as he brushed tears from my face. "What's wrong?"

My skin warmed and buzzed wherever he touched me, and somehow, the bastard calmed me enough to get a handle on my emotions and stop crying.

His tenderness caught me off guard, and the urge to flee, to escape whatever influence he held over me, returned. I liked it better when we were fighting. I could channel the hate to ward off the *tug* toward him.

"I need to go." The longer I stayed, the harder it would be to leave.

"Tell me what's wrong." His words held a plea. "Or do I have to call Killian?" His nose wrinkled.

Dammit, if he called Killian, he would figure out I was leaving and ruin my escape. "Please don't. I'm doing this to protect him." I didn't want to give too much away, but I needed Griffin to let me go.

"How is running out late at night protecting him?" His brows furrowed, and he looked back at Killian's house.

"I thought you couldn't wait until my ass left him." I bit out the words, trying not to let him see how much it had cut me.

"You know I was being a jerk." His phone rang, and he pulled it from his pocket and rejected the call. "Regardless, you can't do that to him. You have to at least say goodbye. Do you know what you disappearing would do to him? He's already lost too many people in his life."

I didn't need this ass clown trying to make me feel bad. He treated people like shit, and he had the audacity to lecture me? I'd already struggled with this decision, so I didn't need him laying it on me too. "People are hunting me. I care about Killian too much to let him get caught in the crossfire."

"The bear shifter would've attacked anyone close to us that day," he growled. "You don't need to feel bad about that."

"I wish it was just him." If I had only one person to worry about, I wouldn't be so nervous or scared. I'd kicked that bear's ass that day all on my own, and I'd been holding back.

"What are you trying to say?" Griffin leaned toward me.

If I wanted to get out of this gracefully, I'd have to bare

my soul to him. "I met Killian only a couple weeks ago." I stopped, needing to prepare myself for the inevitable questions that would come.

Much to my surprise, Griffin didn't rush me. Instead, he patiently waited for me to continue.

"In reality, he probably saved my life." And I'd never even thanked him for that. Another thing I didn't handle correctly. "I almost drowned when I tried to escape a group of men that had chased me from my pack home."

"Drowned?" His body tensed as a low snarl rumbled. "Why were they chasing you?"

"I jumped into the river, trying to hide my scent so they couldn't keep following me. They jumped in after me, and I found an undercurrent that helped me get away, but I almost didn't break free."

"But your pack. Why didn't they help?" he asked. "Is that why you're leaving? To go back to people who abandoned you?"

I laughed without humor. The bleak part of my soul flared. "No, I'll never go back home, but my pack didn't abandon me." I looked skyward at the moon, needing to find comfort in the one thing that I'd never have to give up. "Those men who chased me, they slaughtered my pack before running after me."

His eyes softened as he took a step toward me. "How did you escape?"

I told him the story of how I wasn't there at first and heard the screams. "You see—" I stopped short, bracing myself to spit out the truth. "My pack kept to themselves. We stayed at arm's length from all other supernaturals to keep our identity hidden. But, somehow, some wolves got wind of what we were and that a woman had been born to be the next alpha."

"So they didn't want a woman to lead?" He shook his head. "That doesn't make any sense as to why they'd kill the entire pack then."

"No, they wanted the woman for someone." I averted my gaze toward the ground. "I'm not sure who, but it doesn't matter. They want her to have babies with this man so he can lead her race."

"Why not lead the current pack?" Griffin tilted his head. "You're holding back key pieces of information. I need to understand how you leaving right now, in the middle of the night, protects my best friend."

He was right. I was dancing around the truth when I needed to get straight to the point. "The reason he killed the pack is because none of them—including me—would ever support someone corrupt. I mean, that was the whole reason my people left Shadow City centuries ago."

"There's never been a race that left Shadow City." He glared at me.

Interesting. But then how did Rosemary know about silver wolves? "There was. Your father knew about us. He invited my father to visit around two years ago."

"Your dad..." He *hmm*ed. "Silver hair, like yours?"

"Yes." He must have seen Dad during his visit, but why hadn't his father told him of our existence? Had he, like my father, thought he'd have more time? Atticus's death was starting to seem rather conveniently timed. "Your dad wanted our pack to come back and live in the city." My mind went back in time to the last time I saw my father, and I wrapped my arms around myself. "In fact, with his last breath, my dad told me to go to Shadow City and find Atticus. That he would protect me." I took a deep breath. "That he was an ally of the silver wolves."

Griffin held himself completely still. "Are you saying

silver wolves are real?" He glanced at the moon and then back to me. "And you're the only one still alive—which means you're the alpha they want." He ran his hands through his hair, making it disheveled, which added to his allure. "But your children would only be half silver."

Our legacy was such a well-kept secret that even Rosemary hadn't known this. "No. Any child I have will be a full silver wolf. It's due to the power of the moon."

"And you're running away...because you love Killian."

"Yes. He's already done so much for me. I can't let him wind up dead like the rest of my pack." And here was the grand finale. The last bit of logic that would feed his self-serving side. "And I'll be out of your hair. You won't have to see me again, and you and Killian can go back to the way things were before my messy ass interfered. It'll be like I never existed." Damn, saying that hurt, but I had to seal the deal with him.

"Like you never existed," he said. He scanned my face as if looking for something.

I held my head high, trying to portray confidence. "All you have to do is let me go."

"No." He shook his head. "Absolutely not."

Relief filled me. "Thank—" Wait... he'd said no. "What? Why not?" He hated me.

"Call me selfish, but I don't want you to go." He sighed as his eyes faintly glowed and he took a step closer to me. "I can't."

My body warmed with anticipation as I got closer to him too. My hand itched to touch him, but I held it close to my side.

"Why not?" None of this made any sense. "You've been gone for weeks."

"With the wolf attacks and some council decisions being

made, I had to stay in Shadow City for a little while. Also, Mom needed my help cleaning out Dad's old things. And, if I'm being completely honest, I was trying to stay away from you." He blew out a breath. "I feel something for you, and it's wrong on all types of levels."

My heart pounded. "What do you mean?" I shouldn't ask or encourage him to tell me how he felt, but a part of me had to know if what he felt was similar to what I was feeling.

"I can't get you out of my head, and seeing you try to run away—" He clenched his hands. "And the thought of never seeing you again—" He paused. "That would kill Killian."

We both knew he didn't mean Killian, but our hands were tied. He was with Luna, and Killian and I were supposed to be exclusive. "But I don't want anything to happen... to him."

"I'm the alpha of Shadow City, and if my dad would've protected you, then that's what I'm going to do." He cupped my cheek, and my skin felt like it was on fire. His touch warmed the coldest parts of me inside, and I never wanted him to pull away. "I've been putting off acting like the alpha for too long, and with you here, it's time for me to make some changes."

"I don't want you to change for me." I would never ask that of anyone. "If you aren't ready for that responsibility, then me staying here is a lot to ask."

"You didn't ask." His gaze landed on my lips. "I want to do it. Besides, I'm going to make sure that being with me is the safest place for you."

The air between us charged, and my mind yelled at me to step away. To run as I'd planned. But I was at his mercy. "How so? Someone already threatened me at the university."

"What do you mean?" His hand dropped.

I filled him in on the painting, Rosemary, and the wolf in the woods. "That's what I'm trying to tell you. I'm not paranoid. They've found me here, and that's why I need to run."

He unlocked his phone, and I saw he had over twenty-five missed calls. I hated that I looked, but I couldn't help myself. He cleared the log, pulled up a contact, and began texting. "I'm getting some Shadow City guards over here to protect you with more of Killian's coming. We'll make sure there are four positioned around the house at all times."

My heart quickened. He was taking care of me...and that thrilled me more than it should.

From our spot in the backyard, I watched a taxi pull into Griffin's driveway.

"Oh, hell." He grumbled and lowered his head. "She's fucking insane."

"Who are you talking about?" For him to have that kind of reaction worried me, but surely the group looking for me wouldn't take a taxi and pull into the Shadow City's alpha's driveway.

A car door opened and shut.

"Griffy!" Luna's fingernails-on-a-chalkboard voice called out. She sniffed loudly.

"Ugh, I guesss Griffy and Dove made up." The "p" popped on the last word, emphasizing her inebriated state.

"I'm so sorry about this." He met my eyes. "But you need to go back inside, and I have to deal with my drunken mess."

I'd *bet* he was going to deal with her. I bet he'd deal with her many times. Anger ignited inside of me at the thought. But I had no right. They were together, and sex was part of the equation.

I bet he was damn good at it too. "Yeah, okay. Have fun."

"Fun isn't the word I'd use." He winced. "She's a train wreck."

And yet, he was dating her. Some guys were attracted to people like that.

Luna stumbled in between the houses and stopped when her glazed eyes focused on me.

She was toasted, which meant she'd drunk a ton and had added wolfsbane to the mix. I had no clue why she'd let herself get this sloshed.

"You," she slurred and took a wobbly step in my direction. "Of *course,* he'd be out here with you." She leaned forward, one of her sharp-nailed fingers pointing at me.

Griffin stepped in front of me, blocking me from her view. "What are you doing here, Luna?"

"You din't answer my calls." She shook the finger in his face. "Whut would my daaaddy say?"

Was she threatening him?

"I don't give a flying fuck what he'd say." Griffin crossed his arms, looking unamused. "I'm the alpha, not him."

She laughed. "For suuumone so hawt," she continued, poking him in the chest, "yurrr stupid."

How dare she talk to him like that? I couldn't hold my tongue any longer. "Did you come all this way to insult him?"

Griffin tensed as Luna bared her teeth at me.

"Bish, doan *talk* to me." She waved her hand dismissively at me. "Not *worth* my *time.*"

"Don't talk to her like that." Griffin growled. "You're the one who showed up here wasted. You called me over twenty times, and I didn't answer. Maybe you should've taken the hint."

"You din't git this way 'til *herrr.*" Her bones began to break, and fur sprouted all over her body.

I gasped at the nerve. Was she crazy enough to attack me in this drunken state? I didn't like her, but that didn't mean I wanted to fight her. I wanted her to leave me the hell alone.

Within seconds, she'd shifted into her wolf form, leaving her clothes lying shredded around her paws.

"Luna, what are you doing?" Griffin said sternly. "You need to stand down."

She shook her large wolf head defiantly and ran toward us. Her eyes were locked on my neck.

She intended to kill me.

CHAPTER SIXTEEN

My wolf surged forward, but this time, for protection instead of trying to take control. I allowed the shift to happen as Luna charged at me. My skin tingled as my fur sprouted, and I quickly removed the sheath seconds before my clothes ripped apart and fell from my body.

I hated shifting and ruining my clothes, but she would have an easier time hurting me if I didn't shift too.

"Luna, *stop*," Griffin growled as he stood protectively in front of me. He spread his legs in a fighter pose and tensed his shoulders. "Don't make me force you with my alpha will."

Her wolf made a choking noise that must have been a laugh. She obviously didn't think he had the balls to force her to stop. Given the way Griffin allowed Dick to treat him, it was no wonder she didn't think she had to listen to him. She continued to advance, clearly not concerned about his unveiled threat.

"Fine," he growled as he crouched.

The dumbass was going to get hurt, which infuriated

me. If that bitch injured him in any way, I'd kill her. My wolf howled in agreement.

Luna ran around him and lunged, but in her drunken haze, she miscalculated, and her teeth snapped at Griffin's shoulder instead of me. He held his arms out as if that would prevent injury, but all he did was give her a better target for her teeth.

If my father was here now, he'd have been horrified at how clueless these two shifters were in the art of battle. At least, this time, my head was in the game.

In a bid to keep from adding another kill to my list and end up on the bad side of one of Shadow City's council members, I head-butted Griffin's ass, causing him to stumble out of the way.

"No!" he yelled. "I was handling it!"

If he'd let me focus, I would take down the drunken psycho in seconds.

A snarl ripped from her as she opened her mouth wider, going for my neck. I stood on my hind legs and let her fall, missing her mark completely. She managed to catch herself with her front paws, but they gave out, and she tumbled to the ground.

In order to prevent the fight from continuing, I jumped on her back and placed my teeth at the back of her neck, pressing them into her fur, though not enough to draw blood. If she moved, she'd cause herself injury.

Apparently, that wasn't a deterrent because she thrashed against me, determined to get up. The metallic taste of her blood hit my tongue.

She wasn't thinking clearly and probably didn't even feel the pain. I'd hoped this would be easy, but clearly, I'd been mistaken.

"Luna," Griffin yelled. "Stop it!"

She didn't even pause because she was too desperate to hurt me.

I was going to have to knock her ass *out*. There was no reasoning with her in this state. I jumped off her back, and she got to her feet immediately.

The pool gave me an idea, and I ran toward it. I heard Luna follow, stumbling the entire way. I forced myself to slow down so she wouldn't catch on to my plan. Granted, in her state, that was unlikely, but I knew not to underestimate my opponent.

For the first time in weeks, my mind cleared, and I was able to focus. That would've been nice earlier today with Rosemary and the drawing—and knowing what had caused the change would also be nice.

I'd focus on that later.

When I reached the deep end of the pool, I pivoted and spun out of the way.

Luna tried to stop, scrabbling and teetering on the edge for a second before her body fell over. Her eyes grew huge as she smacked the water, causing a huge splash to hit me and soak my fur.

She came up for air, doggy paddling in the center of the pool. But she treaded water and then sank instead of swimming to the side.

The back door to Killian's house opened, and he ran outside. "What the hell is going on out here?" He first looked at Griffin then me in my wolf form. "Uh..." Concern flicked into his eyes. "Dove, what's going on?"

Like I could answer him in animal form, but his message was clear. Why was I in wolf form in front of Griffin and Luna, of all people?

Luna whimpered, taking his focus off me. I glanced into the pool to find her struggling to stay afloat. I hadn't expected that. I'd figured she could get out—she'd been aware enough to attack me. Her head went under the water again, and it was clear that she wouldn't be able to tread enough water to get to the top.

That wasn't supposed to happen.

"I've got her," Killian yelled as he ran to the pool and jumped in.

As he swam to her, she didn't rise above the surface. I ran to the edge of the pool, whining. The whole point was for me not to kill anyone else, and yet, here she was, almost drowning.

"Hey, he has her." Griffin kneeled beside me. The myrrh scent that was all him filled my nose. Between that and his touch, my wolf and I calmed down. I leaned into him, needing to feel him closer.

Killian wrapped his arms around Luna, keeping her head above water.

My body sagged, and my lungs filled with air once more.

I didn't like her, but that didn't mean I wanted her dead.

The sound of an engine grew louder, and Griffin released me. "We need to get you shifted back to your human form before anyone else sees you."

That was easier said than done, seeing as my clothes were in tatters.

"Come on." Griffin rose, grabbed my sheath and bag and waved me to follow him.

He opened Killian's back door for me. Rushing inside, I ran to Olive's bedroom door, but reality hit me. I'd locked it earlier so that Killian wouldn't barge in and find me gone. At the time, it had seemed like the smart thing to do, but not so much now.

"What's wrong?" Griffin winced as he gestured to

Killian's room. "Go change. Hurry before they come looking for us."

Ugh, this would cause so many questions, but my hands were tied. I trotted to the bedroom I was staying in and whimpered, looking at the top of the door frame where I knew the little metal emergency key was located.

"Whoa! Wait." Griffin's forehead lined with confusion. He followed my gaze to the top of the doorframe then snagged the key and unlocked the door. As he entered the room, he glanced at the skewed sheets on the bed. "You're staying in Olive's room?"

And the questions had already started. I should've put a spare set of clothes in Killian's bedroom in case something like this happened. But I'd never dreamed of *this* happening. At least, I didn't have to attempt to explain it right then since I was in animal form.

Pushing past him, I dug in the closet, not finding a damn thing to wear.

His chuckle forced me to turn around to find my bag on the floor and unzipped. Not looking at him, I rummaged through the bag carefully grabbing with my mouth jeans, bra, and white shirt.

Once I gathered my things, I turned to find Griffin sitting on the bed, watching me. One corner of his mouth tipped upward, and he looked almost pleased.

In other words, he looked drop-dead sexy, and the *tug* inside me seemed to coil and tighten.

Car doors slammed shut, alerting me that the guards had arrived. Welcoming the reprieve, I rushed out the door, not wanting to attempt to try to get him to leave my room. The way he was acting, he wouldn't budge, waiting instead for a show. So, I slipped into the bathroom to get some privacy.

My body tingled as I pushed my wolf away, and soon, I was standing back on two legs. I glanced in the mirror and, for a second, felt almost like myself, which was a welcome change. My emotions were more centered, and likewise, the dark circles under my eyes that had been there not even an hour ago had vanished. The shift and the moon must have done wonders for my mental stability. In fact, the overwhelming feelings of being alone that I'd previously entertained weren't suffocating at the moment.

I sagged against the dark granite sink and looked around the large bathroom. Beige tile complemented the light yellow walls. The tub and toilet sat against one wall, and across from the sink was a large linen closet that Killian kept stocked with towels. I grabbed a fresh hand towel, splashed my face with water, and patted it dry.

I could faintly hear the guards talking with Killian. They'd be coming in soon, so I quickly dressed.

Griffin knocked on the bathroom door. "Are you okay in there?"

His voice made goosebumps break out across my arms. Lord, I had it bad, but I had to keep my head on straight. "Yeah, I'm almost done." I put my bra on and pulled the white shirt down over my jeans. I took a moment and closed my eyes. There was no telling what kind of state Luna would be in, and I hoped that she didn't try to kick my ass again. I felt bad for dumping her in the pool since she'd obviously been even more drunk than I realized.

I heard Griffin walk down the hallway. The farther he moved away from me, the more desperate I felt to get close to him again. This couldn't continue to happen. I didn't need to get to the point where I relied on him.

The back door opened. "What the hell happened out

there?" I heard Killian rasp as four sets of footsteps entered behind him. "And why are there Shadow City guards here?"

I grabbed some bath towels from the linen closet and then ran into the living room. As I expected, wolf Luna was soaking wet. Killian was carrying her in his arms past the guards as water dripped all over the wood floor.

"Here," I said and held my hands out to take her from Killian so he could dry off.

"Uh, hell no," Griffin growled and took the towels away from me, the warmth of his body making the hairs rise on my arms as I swayed toward him. *Dammit.* "You're wearing a white shirt, and I'll be damned if you're giving them a show."

My cheeks burned, and I almost wanted to take her anyway to prove a point.

Almost.

But I didn't want to entertain the new men, so I let it go.

However, when Griffin took Luna from Killian, intense jealousy slammed into me. The irrational anger that surged through me when he touched her scared the shit out of me and luckily woke me up enough to keep my head in check. The girl almost died. I had to remember that.

Killian took a towel from me and dried off as I threw the two other towels onto the floor, trying to wipe up the water mess before his floors were ruined.

"What should I do with her?" Griffin wrinkled his nose.

There was only one option. "Put her in the bathtub, and I'll get her some clothes in case she shifts back."

He followed my instructions, which surprised me. Normally, he was more combative.

"Once again, why the hell were you outside when you were supposed to be safely sleeping in bed, and why are there four guards here?" Killian's dark eyes locked on me and then glanced at the four guards standing at the back door.

I sucked in a breath, remembering the scents of the guards, and was about to tell Killian what I could when Griffin joined us back in the kitchen area. He filled in Killian and the guards on my wolf stalker and everything that had been happening.

Well... almost everything. Not the silver wolf part.

"We'll secure the perimeter," a bald-headed guard said. "No one will get by."

"Good, I'll stay here with them." Griffin motioned to Killian and me. "Let me know if you need anything, and I want you reporting in every hour."

"Yes, alpha." The oldest guard nodded and headed out the door.

When the four of them left, Killian rubbed his arms. "You were running away?" He sounded hurt as he touched my shoulder, making me meet his gaze.

"I don't want anything to happen to you." He had to understand that. "Think about it—if someone was hunting you, and they were willing to kill me in order to succeed, what would *you* do? And I couldn't tell you goodbye. If I tried, I knew I wouldn't leave." I felt like a huge asshole. If he was this upset from me contemplating it, what would've happened if I'd managed to go through with it?

"It doesn't matter." Killian stepped toward me, his face set with determination. "You are one of the most important people in my life now, and I refuse to let some assholes take that from me. Do you understand?"

"Yes. I'm sorry. But I wasn't trying to hurt you." I wanted him to know that. "It was just...every time I closed my eyes, I saw you dead, along with everyone else I love."

Killian pulled me into his arms and kissed the top of my

head. "I know that feeling too, but you can't get rid of me. Okay?"

A deep growl emanated from Griffin as he stepped closer, pulling Killian's attention away from me.

"Dude, what the hell?" Killian frowned.

Griffin must have been feeling the same thing that came over me when I watched him carry Luna away. I pulled out of Killian's arms, trying to calm the situation.

"It's been a long night." Griffin rasped, as if trying to smooth out his reaction.

"Let me go get Luna to drink water and eat something, or she's going to feel like hell in the morning."

"And I'm going to dry off." Killian picked at the shirt that was plastered to his chest. "I'll change and come back out here to make her something to eat."

He had the better end of the deal. I watched him walk off, feeling even worse that I'd almost left without saying goodbye.

I'd taken one step toward Olive's bedroom to get Luna some clothes when Griffin cut me off.

His hazel eyes glowed, emphasizing the flecks of green as he came close enough that his minty breath hit my face. "If you leave, I will find you. I will use every resource I have until you're back here where you belong." He tucked a piece of hair behind my ear, which made a shiver run through me. "If you so much as *breathe* the wrong way, one of the guards will alert me. There's no escaping me now, Dove."

My breath hitched, and my body grew warm all over. I never dreamed possessive words would turn me on, but here I stood, wrong.

CHAPTER SEVENTEEN

The sweet scent of arousal wafted from my betraying body. I had to shut down whatever was brewing between us before he thought I was down for a one-night stand. I still hadn't changed my mind about that, and to be honest, if I let myself go there with him, I wasn't sure I'd be able to pick up the pieces afterward.

He had a hold on my mind, body, and soul.

I despised him for it.

A cocky smile appeared on his sculpted face. He knew *exactly* what he was doing to me.

Humiliated, I pivoted to walk around him, but he countered, staying in front of me. He placed a hand on my waist, and the *tug* grew even stronger.

"What are you trying to prove?" I asked quietly. "My boyfriend is in the other room."

"Boyfriend?" He stepped closer.

His scent overloaded my mind, turning me into a bundle of nerves. His own sweet scent slammed into me, making it clear I had an effect on him too.

"Hmmm..." he whispered as he placed a finger under my chin, tilting my head upward.

I licked my lips as my brain stopped working. "What?" I couldn't remember what he'd asked.

"Killian is your *boyfriend*?" His nose wrinkled as his hands wrapped around my waist.

"We're exclusive." I nodded my head. He already knew this. Why was he asking the question again?

His face fell, but he was close enough now that his chest brushed against me. "Are you attracted to him like you are to me?"

There was absolutely no way to get out of this gracefully, and he knew that. The asshole was setting me up to admit it either with my words or the stench of a lie. "It doesn't matter." I somehow found the strength to step back, putting distance between us, despite my body and my wolf warring inside me.

"Really?" He chuckled. "Because it kind of does to me." He moved right back into my space and kissed me, catching me by surprise. His lips were soft and warm, so damn inviting. My body hummed, wanting more of him.

When he slipped his tongue into my mouth, his delicious taste overwhelmed my senses, and a moan escaped from my throat. Thankfully, the noise startled me enough to snap me out of the moment.

I pushed him in the chest, hard. "Stop," I said as instinct and emotion warred inside me. A large part of me wanted to kiss him again and let him do things to me that had never been done before, but another part of me felt so much guilt. Even though Killian and I were only friends, we had promised to be exclusive. I'd broken his trust with my momentary weakness.

"Why?" he asked, licking my taste from his lips.

"I'm with your *best friend*." He knew why. We had this conversation not even five minutes ago. "You can't kiss me when I'm with him."

Griffin shrugged. "Break up with him."

"And have a fling with you?" Oh, look. His douchebag side was coming out again. This I could handle. I circled him slowly, preparing to get away to help Luna. "You're saying you would do that to your best friend and to Luna?"

I had never despised someone as much as I wanted him before. I wanted to slap him and kiss him at the same time.

"I wouldn't be doing anything to them." He countered my movements, remaining close. "So, I'm going to ask—"

A whimper escaped from the bathroom, alerting us that Luna was stirring.

For the first time ever, I was ecstatic to hear her. I pushed past him and rushed into the bathroom. Anything that would give me distance from Griffin so my mind could focus once more.

She hacked as she lay, head raised, on the plastic floor of the tub. Her brown fur was drenched, and her head bobbed like she was dizzy.

I'd never been in that condition before, but Zoe had, one night when her parents had gone out of town. She'd invited me and a few more people to hang out, and they'd all gotten so drunk they were puking all over the floor. I refused to join them because Dad would've lost his shit—alphas didn't behave stupidly.

Wow, if only he could see me now. Behaving stupidly was all that I'd done, despite not meaning to.

Rubbing a paw over her face, Luna groaned.

"Let me grab you some clothes, and I'll be right back." I said the words, though I doubted she'd care. I remembered what it felt like to almost drown. Maybe being intoxicated on top of it was a blessing in disguise for her.

I hurried into Olive's room and grabbed a pair of black sweatpants that had Juicy written on the ass and a matching top. It looked like an outfit Luna would wear herself, so at least there was that. If I'd had clothes to spare, I would've made her wear mine out of spite, so it was probably a good thing that I had only a couple of pairs of boring pants to my name.

When I turned back toward the door, I found Griffin standing against the wall, watching me. His eyes were so dark I couldn't see any of the green. His smoldering expression sent chills up and down my body.

Focus, Sterlyn. He could break you, and you're already struggling to keep your shit together.

I tried to ignore him as I marched past, heading back to Luna, but it was so damn *hard*. The *tug* was now almost a *yank*, and every one of my cells seemed to be on fire. The need that surged through me nearly overwhelmed me.

Killian's door opened, and he stepped into the hallway. He frowned but didn't say a thing, which made me feel even more guilty for the stolen kiss.

"You need any help?" he asked.

"Wow," Griffin said sarcastically. "Is that your way of telling Dove that you want to see other people naked?"

"Dude," Killian said as he faced his best friend. "What the hell? I didn't mean that at all!"

"Are you sure?" Griffin lifted both hands. "Because you know she's trying to get Luna to shift and get dressed, so I'm not sure how that could be taken any other way."

Oh, great. They were going to have a pissing match. I didn't want any part of that. "I'm good. Thanks." I was a little shocked that Griffin didn't volunteer to help get Luna changed, but I didn't overthink it. I despised the idea of him being near her anyway.

I left them scowling at one another and entered the bathroom, shutting the door behind myself. I laid the clothes on the bathroom sink and walked over to her.

This time, she was sitting with her wolfish head lying against the side of the cool plastic. When she sensed me, she turned toward me and let out a low growl.

Great. For all I knew, she was going to try to attack me again. "Come on, you need to get some food and water into you. Otherwise, you'll get sick again." I tried using a nice but not over-the-top tone with her.

She huffed and tossed her head.

I had no clue what she was trying to tell me to do, but if I was a betting woman, I'd say she was telling me to go to Hell. "I'm trying to help you."

She growled again in response and stood on shaky legs. Her eyes flicked from the door to me and back to the door.

Of course, she didn't want my help. "Okay, I'll go outside. I put the clothes on the sink in case you want to shift." I pointed to them. "Let me know if you need anything." When I opened the door, she huffed, making it clear that she wouldn't ask for my help even if she needed it.

Fine, let her struggle. I refused to kiss her ass.

When I stepped back into the hallway, Killian and Griffin stood in the living room, still glaring at one another. The drama was getting overwhelming. At this point, all I wanted to do was get Luna out of here and go to bed.

"You can't stand it that I got her first." Killian sneered. "Well, too bad. You need to stop sniffing around her."

Great, they were fighting over me. The last thing I wanted to do was come between the two of them. No girl should ever do that.

"If I hadn't been sniffing, she would've slipped away tonight since you obviously weren't paying attention to her." Griffin lifted his chin, daring his friend to disagree. "So maybe a 'thank you' is in order."

Oh, dear God. Did Griffin think that logic would work? If anything, he'd made the entire situation worse. I decided to intervene before things got even more upside down. "Hey, you two, cut it out." I stepped over to them, avoiding Killian's gaze. Each passing second caused more guilt to settle over me. "We have too much going on to be at each other's throats."

"Now that I can agree with." Killian grabbed my hand and pulled me beside him.

Griffin bared his teeth, making it clear that he didn't like Killian touching me.

Dammit. Luna was his girlfriend, and he'd kissed me. Not only had I betrayed Killian, but what did that say about Griffin? He had way too much influence over me. Hell, he got me to agree to stay.

We couldn't let our emotions get the best of us. "The entire day has been a shit show." That was the only way I knew to explain it. "All of our emotions are everywhere, and between me almost leaving and Luna almost drowning, we all need a time out." I dropped Killian's hand, not wanting to antagonize Griffin more than he already was, which was way too telling. I should be more worried about Killian than him, but I'd analyze that later. Right then, I needed space. "I'm going to my room for a second." I grimaced, realizing that this would lead to more questions.

"Speaking of which." Griffin pointed a finger at the two of us. "If you two are together, why is she sleeping in your sister's room?"

The bathroom door opened, and Luna stomped down

the hallway. When she saw the three of us, she sighed with what looked like relief. She weaved over to Griffin and threw her arms around him. "Thank you fur shaving my liiife."

I clenched my hands into fists as I worked to keep myself from grabbing her by the hair. I wanted to yank her the fuck away from Griffin, and I hated that she got to smell his delicious scent.

"That wasn't me." He removed her arms from him and took a step back. He wiped the spot on his shirt that she'd gotten soaking wet from her hair. "You can thank Killian for that."

"What?" she asked and blinked, turning to face Killian and me. When her gaze landed on me, rage filled her eyes. "Thissiz all yur fault." She shook her head hard from side to side. "You *attacked* me, and yur fur was siiilver."

Great. Even drunk, she remembered that I had silver fur, but not that it wasn't Griffin who saved her. She had it out for me, and I had no clue why. "You think I had silver fur?" I forced laughter, trying to make it sound like that was the funniest thing I'd ever heard.

Her face turned sour, and she ran her fingers through her hair. They got caught halfway through where there was a large knot. "I doan feel so good."

Yeah, I bet she didn't.

"Come on." Griffin walked to the back door. "Let's get you taken care of."

Her eyes lit up at his words while pure rage coursed through me. My breathing quickened, drawing Killian's eyes to me.

Way to go, Sterlyn

"'Kay," she said eagerly and looped her arm through Griffin's.

His face twisted, but he didn't remove himself from her clutches.

I wasn't sure if that was better or worse. At least, he didn't seem to be enjoying the contact, but he was letting her touch him. What if he continued to let her touch him when they got back to his house?

My wolf surged forward, howling with hurt and anger, and I clenched my fists so hard that my nails dug into my palm. However, it was enough to cause some rationale to flit back into my mind. What the hell was going on with me?

"I'll come back in the morning," Griffin said as he opened the door. "And I'll let you know the guards' schedule." He winked at me before leading Luna out the door and shutting it behind them.

The asshole *winked* at me as he was taking another girl to his house. What the *hell*? And why did it enrage me so much? He'd kissed me, and I told him no. If anything, that kind of made this partially my fault, but I'd made a promise to Killian.

"Hey, what's wrong?" Killian asked, and he touched my arm.

Like I would be answering that question. I couldn't admit to him how I felt about his best friend for so many reasons, although, granted, he probably had an inkling based on the scents of our attraction earlier. But Griffin was a player, and I had to remember that.

"Dove?" He squeezed my arm comfortingly. "Are you okay?"

"No." I wasn't okay for so many reasons. "My whole life keeps falling apart. Right when I felt some semblance of normal, I find a painting of me near a dumpster. Then I confirm Rosemary's suspicions while letting some random wolf overhear me admit to everything!" He already knew all this, but I couldn't stop. "*Then* I try to leave and get caught by that ass-clown—" I pointed toward Griffin's house "—and then his drunken girlfriend attacks me. There is no part of this that's okay." Not to mention the kiss, which I would have to tell Killian about.

"Look, I get that we're more friends than lovers." Killian placed his hands on my shoulders, making me look at him. "But Griffin isn't good for you. This isn't me being jealous— I'm telling you as a friend. He doesn't want to settle down, and he makes a point to prove it at every opportunity. I don't want to see you get hurt. He has a way of making a girl feel special, and he seems to be focusing that on you, which pisses me off because we're best friends, and you're supposed to be my girl."

His words were like a slap in the face, even though I already knew that they were all true. And here it was. I had to tell Killian the truth. I'd made a promise to him, and I broke it. I had to take the blame and deal with the consequences. I didn't want to ruin their friendship. "Killian, I need to tell you something."

He tilted his head and inhaled sharply. "What?"

"Griffin and I kissed."

CHAPTER EIGHTEEN

A tense silence swallowed us whole.

His jaw twitched as he processed my words, and I braced myself for the inevitable blow.

"Who initiated it?" Killian huffed. "Was it him?" He started pacing.

That was the exact question I'd hoped he wouldn't ask. There was already a ton of tension between them, and I didn't want to cause more, but I'd broken my promise to Killian and had to tell him. "What matters is that it ended almost as soon as it began, and I'm so sorry that I betrayed your trust." In reality, the kiss had lasted seconds, but I could still feel his lips on mine.

"So...he kissed you." Killian stopped and stared at me. "Dove, he's bad news."

Something snapped inside me. "He brought four guards here to protect us. How is that bad news?"

His brows furrowed as he sighed. "No, I mean he's bad news to girls. Look, apart from his dating habits, Griffin is a great guy and a good friend. Well, at least he was before he kissed you." He laughed without humor. "Either way, he has made it abundantly clear that he doesn't want to settle down, and I don't want you to get hurt."

He was right. Somehow, I *had* opened myself up to getting hurt by Griffin, but I couldn't help it. No matter how loud my head screamed, my heart and wolf wanted to be next to him. I was at war inside, and my brain was losing. "No, I get it. He did hit on me horribly my first day in the coffee shop."

"I'm not trying to be ugly or mean." Killian touched my arm. "But I'm afraid he did that because I claimed you first. And don't forget that he left with Luna."

That was like a punch to my gut, but sometimes the truth was hard to hear. Everything he said made sense, but it didn't erase the crazy connection I had with Griffin. "I know."

"Look, I know you're helping me out with the pretend relationship thing, and if your fated mate or some other great guy came along, we'd end the ruse immediately. But Griffin is not the one." He kissed my forehead. "And I don't want to see you get hurt more than you already have, losing your family and pack."

"Not to mention that I have some wacko threatening me." I had to stop thinking about Griffin and what he and Luna were probably doing right at this moment.

The thought of them having sex, or God knew what else, kept trying to creep into my mind, making me want to march over there and kick Griffin in the nads. At least then, he'd be hurting and thinking of me.

Whoa. That was a violent thought. And why did I care if he wanted to be with Luna? I needed to keep my head level.

And that right there spoke volumes.

My reaction to Griffin wasn't rational, which confirmed

my nagging fear. "Look, I want to be honest with you. Griffin and I... we have a strange connection, and even though it's probably a *very* bad idea, seeing as he left with Luna... I need to explore it."

"Dove—" His face pinched.

"I get it." Boy did I ever, but after going two weeks without seeing Griffin, my heart hurt from wanting to be close to him. "But I'd rather have your blessing than do something behind your back."

"All I'm saying is, you deserve someone who's going to treat you with respect, loyalty, and kindness." Killian hugged me. "And if this is something you need to explore..." He sighed and ran a hand down his face. "Then you have my blessing. But if he hurts you, I will kick his ass and not have anything to do with him anymore."

I chuckled, but it sounded a little watery. "I'm so glad that I met you. You're like a piece of my family I didn't realize was missing."

"And I kinda love you too." He pulled back and arched an eyebrow. "But no more running away, or you *will* be sleeping with me in my bed. Got it?"

"Maybe I'll misbehave then." I winked, totally messing with him.

"Yeah, yeah." He rolled his eyes. "But seriously. The fact that you were planning to run away hurts. We're family. If you go, then you better take me."

"But you have your life here, and your pack." Although... he didn't talk about his pack much, now that I thought about it.

"It's my dad's pack. All I've done is let them down and allow them to lose their alpha before his time." He frowned.

I hated that he felt responsible, but that was something he'd have to work out himself. "You know that you're the alpha, and you haven't stepped down for a reason. I see how Sierra and Carter look at you, and it isn't with hate or disgust. They love and respect you, which shows you're doing something right."

"Maybe, but I'm not ready." He yawned. "Look, I'm exhausted. I'm going to bed. We've got to get to the university early tomorrow."

Shit, I'd forgotten all about work. I was going to be dead on my feet. "You're right. I'm sorry about all this." If I hadn't tried to sneak out, then none of tonight would've happened, including the kiss.

"No, it's actually a good thing." Killian nodded toward the back door. "We now have four guards protecting us, so we'll know if anyone tries anything."

That was true. "Yeah, Griffin said that I'd be safer here than on the run by myself."

"I hate to admit it, but he's right." Killian yawned again, and I heard his jaw crack. "Now let's go get some rest."

We walked to the bedrooms, and he opened his door all the way. "I'm leaving this open to make sure I catch you next time you try to do something—"

"Smart? Selfless?" I interjected. "Loving?"

"Foolish." He squeezed my arm tenderly. "Good night."

"Night." I left my door cracked open too and crawled into bed. Surprisingly, I fell right to sleep.

Murmurs from the kitchen woke me.

"Sir, she needs to stay here and not go to the university." A voice I didn't recognize spoke. "It'll be too hard to try to keep her safe with all those people around her."

Sir? Was Griffin here already? I glanced at the clock. It was almost seven.

"You're right," Killian's voice replied. "That coffee shop is always busy. I'll link with Carter and let him know and then run by and make sure everything is okay with the painting."

Yeah, I had to be part of the conversation about what I'd be doing all day. I got up and made my way toward the voices.

A tall man who had to be in his mid-thirties stood in front of Killian. He had his arms crossed, emphasizing his muscular biceps through his black shirt. He had two guns strapped around his waist, and his amber eyes homed in on me. A blackish eyebrow arched high enough that his matching longish hair hid it. "I take it this is Dove?" His attention went back to Killian.

Yeah, that wasn't going to happen. I could answer questions about myself just fine. "Yes, I am. And you are?"

"Lucas," he said curtly. "I'm part of Killian's pack. We were discussing your safety."

"Were you?" I tried to keep the sarcasm out of my voice but failed miserably. "I didn't realize that either of you could make decisions on my behalf." I probably would've been willing if the asshole hadn't laid out what I was going to do without discussing it with me.

"It wasn't quite like that." Killian glowered at the man. "Lucas made some very good points about you staying home. The coffee shop will be so packed with people that anyone could slip in and get to you. It'll be hard to keep an eye on everyone without making it obvious that you're under guard."

Establishing security measures would be hard; I couldn't argue with them there. "Carter will be pissed." But honestly, I didn't want to go back there yet. Call me a coward, but taking a day to recover might be a good thing. A day to work through my issues, instead of continually making poor decisions. I hadn't sat back and reflected on anything.

"I'll handle him." Killian winked. "Don't worry about that. And I better get moving because I wanted to check on the paint job I did and make sure nothing bled through."

"Is there anything else we need to discuss, sir?" Lucas asked.

"Nope, make sure no one gets inside to hurt her." Killian patted my arm as he walked by, leaving me alone with the guard.

I didn't like being around people I didn't know, but I couldn't be rude when this guy was protecting me.

"Well, I better get back outside." Lucas opened the door to the porch. "Let us know if you need anything."

"Will do." I strolled over to the couch and picked up the remote then turned on the television.

I'D BEEN THERE by myself for all of thirty minutes, and I was already restless. I flopped around on the couch, trying to get comfortable, but nothing helped.

Footsteps pounded on the back porch and the door opened once more. Between the rhythm of the feet and the *tug* that took hold, I already knew who it was...and I hated it.

Despite him not being the massive creep he'd appeared to be the other day, I still wasn't thrilled that fate had chosen *him* of all people. He'd left with Luna last night, so what did that say about our connection? Something had to be wrong, and I had to be misreading the situation.

The problem was after tossing and turning all night, I was pretty damn sure I knew what this overwhelming, horrifying connection was.

Griffin had to be my fated mate.

Which didn't make any sense and shouldn't be possible. In fact, I hated that the thought had even crossed my mind, and yet...it resonated with my soul.

Of course, he'd show up now, after Luna must have left. The anger inside me at what they might have done put me in a combative mood.

When he stepped into the living room, I somehow prevented myself from getting up and running toward him. He looked fresh with his hair gelled to the side and his maroon shirt fitting him like a second skin. He placed his hands in his jeans pockets as he scanned me from head to toe.

My body warmed.

"Hey, you," he drawled as he sauntered over to me. "A little birdie told me that you were staying home today."

"I know that little birdie wouldn't be Killian." It had to be one of the guards. "He's pissed at you."

"Oh?" He looked amused. "How come?"

I sat up, surprised at his cavalier attitude. "Because I told him that we kissed."

He shrugged and sat next to me, throwing his arm over my shoulders. "I'm thinking there is more to the story between you and Killian."

"Are you trying to be funny?" I scooted away from him, needing him not to touch me. I lost my mind that way. "As far as you know, he and I are dating." I wanted to see how he reacted to my words.

He smirked. "I don't think that you really are. I would even go as far as to say you two view each other more like siblings than anything."

"What?" I said in a way too high-pitched voice. "I don't have to explain anything to you." Shit, why would he say that? Were we not convincing? "Besides, it's not just Killian that's part of this equation. Speaking of which, how is *Luna*?"

"Probably hungover as hell." He laughed. "Her dad was not pleased. He called me, apologizing profusely when she got home."

"Well, I'm sure she made up for the inconvenience she caused you many times over." I crossed my arms and turned my head, cheeks burning, refusing to meet his eyes. I didn't want to see what was reflecting back at me.

"What are you talking about?" He sounded bewildered. "When I left here, I dropped her off at her house and immediately left."

My heart leaped with joy, and I told it to sit the hell down. I wasn't going to fall for the innocent-playboy act. I stood, needing to get away from him, but he grabbed my waist and brought me down beside him, the *tug* pulling us together.

"I asked you a question," he rasped.

"She's your girlfriend." I inhaled sharply, trying to keep my act together. I wanted to explore things with him—I couldn't help but want to be with my fated mate—but not while he was with someone else. "It's fine. But you shouldn't be here with me alone."

"Why the hell would you think she's my girlfriend?" he asked as he cupped my face and turned me to look at him.

I expected to see malice, contempt, or something, but instead, I found concern. His eyes were tender, and the cocky man I'd met that day in the coffee shop appeared to be gone.

"Because she told me that, during those weeks when you were gone, you'd been spending them with her." That conversation had devastated me, even though I didn't like to admit it. "That she'd been able to get you to settle down sooner than she expected."

"Are you fucking serious?" he snarled. "She's such a bitch. Killian had her pegged all along."

"So you aren't together?" I wanted to take that back because the answer was way too important to me. But there it was, hanging out there for him to answer and potentially to break me.

He smiled. "No, but she did have part of that right." He leaned so his lips hovered over mine. "For the first time ever, I do want to settle down."

My heart raced, and butterflies took flight in my stomach. "That's funny, after all I've heard about you."

"Oh, everything you heard is true, but this silver-haired girl walked into my life, turning everything upside down." He brushed his lips against mine. "The first time I met her, she challenged me, infuriated me, and was so damn alluring. The first moment I laid eyes on her and she cut through all my bullshit, I was a goner."

"You expect me to believe that?" My head didn't believe him, but my heart and wolf did. The awful stench of a lie was missing. My wolf whimpered, wanting to get closer. "You fought with me constantly and disappeared until last night. You didn't even come into the shop."

"When I lost my dad, it was the worst day of my entire life," he said as he took my hand. "And I swore I would never grow close to anyone else again. But then you came here, and not only did I care for you, but I fell for you so damn hard that the thought of losing you makes me insane."

Happiness surged through me stealing my breath. I never thought I'd even feel a fraction of this ever again, but that was the kind of effect this man had on me.

"So you ran?" He and I were more alike than I'd thought.

"Yeah, but every day, the urge to see you again got stronger and stronger. Watching you with Killian would have killed me." He turned his body fully toward me. "But yesterday, I couldn't stay away any longer. It was like something pulled me back here in the nick of time. I'd only been home a few minutes before something told me you were outside. And there you were, running away."

"Griffin—" I started, but he placed a finger over my lips.

"Please let me get this out." His irises darkened to a brown.

I nodded, wanting to hear what he had to say.

"Between you confiding your secret to me and Luna trying to hurt you, I knew my heart was done for. That I would have to watch you with Killian, from the sidelines." He rubbed his thumb against my wrist. "But then I came into the house to help you get shifted back and realized that, not only are you sleeping in Olive's room alone, but you don't love Killian in the way I feared you did, and I didn't need to worry about betraying my best friend any longer. You are fair game."

"What are you talking about?" There was no way he could've known that Killian and my relationship was based on pure friendship.

"Because I found this." He pulled a piece of paper from his pocket and unfolded it.

My breath caught as he showed me the letter I'd written

to Killian. Griffin did know everything. "That's why you kissed me."

"Yup." He waggled his brows. "The only thing standing between you and me wasn't a problem after all. I wouldn't be betraying my best friend, and I had to see if you felt the same way about me."

"And what did you determine?" My breath caught as I looked at his lips.

"That you do." He kissed me, not holding back any longer. My stomach fluttered, and my head grew dizzy as his tongue slipped inside my mouth. His hands went to my waist, dragging me onto his lap. He began to whisper against my lips.

"At first, I thought it couldn't be possible, that this feeling was lust. Each time I see you... touch you... kiss you, I can't focus on anything else." He pulled back, and his eyes stared into my soul as he whispered, "We're fated mates. Tell me that you feel it?" He peppered kisses down my face.

His words crumbled every wall I'd built up around my heart. Maybe he'd been a player before, but everything inside told me that we'd changed each other. The *tug* between our souls was painfully blissful, as if we needed to connect to make us whole. "I feel the same way."

I straddled him, needing to be closer, but I still couldn't get close enough. My body caught fire as I slipped my tongue into his mouth, and he matched me stroke for stroke. The sweet scent of arousal coursed between us.

Between his minty taste and his smell, my head swam in a way I never wanted to end. I moaned when his fingertips brushed the bare skin of my stomach, and my need for him slammed through me.

His hand slipped under my shirt, cupping my breast as I rocked against him. I had no clue what I was doing, but he bucked against me, making me feel as if I was doing something right.

As I kissed down his neck, he sighed. "Wait. We can't do this."

The rejection stung as I pulled back. "What? But I thought—"

"I *want* to." He removed his hands from under my shirt and growled. "But you deserve better than this. I don't want to take you in Killian's house while he's out. You deserve to be courted and pampered. I want to give you all of my attention and go back to an empty house so we can take our time in my bed." He kissed me and ran his fingers through my hair. "I want our first time together to be the best memory possible because it'll be the start of our whole life together."

"You do want this?" The tug had become an overwhelming leaping sensation that made me yearn for every inch of him. For him to want to wait made me fall even more.

"There's no doubt in my mind." He gently pressed his lips to mine. "So, Dove, what are you doing tonight?"

"Sterlyn," my name fell from my lips.

"What?" His brows furrowed. "Sterlyn?"

"It's my real name." No one had called me that in so long. "I didn't tell Killian my name, so he started calling me Dove."

"It's beautiful." He brushed his lips against mine. "So, what are you doing tonight, Sterlyn?"

"Pretty sure some desperate alpha is going to wind up showing up at my door, begging me to be his for the night," I teased him, unable to stop myself. In this moment, I was so damn happy.

"You better make him grovel." He sighed and leaned his forehead against mine.

The garage door rumbled open, indicating that Killian had arrived home.

"Well, it's a good thing we didn't take things further now," Griffin said as he pecked my lips. "I guess there's no time like the present to inform my protective best friend I'll be taking his sister out tonight."

I tensed. Griffin acted confident that this was all going to work out, but I wasn't so sure.

CHAPTER NINETEEN

I jumped to my feet, not wanting Killian to walk in on me straddling his best friend.

Oh, dear God. That sounded horrible, and what Killian had said to me last night about Griffin not being the right guy for me made this entire situation surreal. But I'd been honest with him, and he knew that I wanted to explore things with Griffin. Granted, I was pretty sure completing the mate bond with him tonight wasn't *exploring* so much as committing to each other.

My gut screamed that something uncomfortable was imminent, but this was something Griffin and I should do together. Either way, Griffin had become determined that I was going to be his.

The thought both thrilled and terrified me.

Griffin chuckled as he stood next to me, taking my hand.

A pause in Killian's footsteps told me he'd figured out that Griffin was here. A low growl emanated from him as he hurried into the room and stopped short.

"What's going on?" Killian straightened his shoulders as he stared at his best friend.

"I came over to ask Ster—*Dove* out tonight." Griffin leaned closer to me.

"Griffin, she's important to me," Killian said. "I don't want to see her get hurt."

I hated that these two were arguing over me again.

"That's fair. And I know I've been behaving like an asshole, but that's changing from now on." Griffin lifted our joined hands. "She's my fated mate."

Killian closed his eyes and exhaled. He looked up and met first my eyes, then Griffin's. "I can't stand between something special like this, but no more fucking games." Killian's shoulders sagged. "She's lost so much already."

"There won't be." I straightened my shoulders, standing tall beside Griffin. I couldn't let him be the only one fighting for us. "I told you last night that I felt the connection. It's real."

Killian's jaw tightened as he glared at his friend. "Remember when you told me you're not the 'settling down' type of guy?"

Wow, I figured this was going to be tense, but I hadn't expected Killian to call out his friend directly. Though I guessed I shouldn't be surprised that he was protective of me after all we'd gone through.

"Yeah, I remember, but ever since she walked into our lives, I've been pulled in her direction." Griffin faced me. "That damn *tug* had me going into that coffee shop the first day without Luna having to nag me. Then I saw the most beautiful girl standing behind the counter, and I froze—then acted like a dirtbag."

"I can't argue with you there." If he wanted me to

comfort him, he'd come to the wrong person. He had been an asshole that day.

"He hits on every woman that way." Killian dropped his backpack on the floor and locked eyes with me. "He tries humping anything with two legs when the mood strikes."

"This is *different*," Griffin rasped. "When I realized what she was to you, it drove me insane. Every time you touched her, I wanted to punch the shit out of you. That's one of the reasons I left for so long. I had a ton of stuff that I needed to do with Mom and the council, but also, I couldn't stand to see her with you, and I didn't want to be tempted to interfere. You're my best friend. If she made you happy, I had to leave in order to respect that."

Killian rolled his eyes and crossed his arms. "Dude."

But I wasn't sure if that was the only thing. Maybe his reasoning was a tad bit selfish. "Griffin and I decided to pursue this, but know you will never lose either of us."

"If you break up, I will." Killian hung his head, but then he stalked over and hugged me. "You're my family now, and I don't want to risk that."

Griffin growled but didn't do more than that. "Man, I would *never* hurt her. I know I have a bad track record, but I'm serious about Dove. She's it for me."

"If you were being all noble and left out of respect for the relationship that you thought she and I had, then why did you come back last night?" Killian released me and faced his friend.

"I couldn't stay away any longer. Hell, Mom told me if I didn't stop frowning and snapping, she would personally put me in Shadow City's jail. I could barely pay attention to the council meetings because all I wanted to do was come back here to her." Griffin sighed. "I wasn't going to act on it. I wanted to see her for a few minutes to subdue whatever this urge was inside me. But then the whole Luna thing happened, and I found this note that our little runaway left you." He pulled the piece of paper back out of his pocket.

I inhaled and held my breath, guessing how Killian would react.

"Note?" Killian asked and took it from him. His eyes scanned it, and I saw when realization sank in. "*This* was how you were telling me goodbye?"

"We've gone through this." I didn't want to talk about it again. "I couldn't say it to your face because I wouldn't have been able to leave. But I had to make sure you knew I left of my own free will—and how much your friendship means to me."

"Don't make her feel bad," Griffin said as he touched my arm. "She thought she was doing the right thing."

Killian's jaw tightened, and he folded my letter up and put it into his back pocket. "Can I talk to you alone for a minute?" He pointed at Griffin.

"Whatever you have to say, you can say it in front of Dove." Griffin tightened his hold on me. "She and I are a package deal."

"No, it's fine." Griffin was already acting like we were together, and though I loved the sound of it, I had to make sure Killian was okay with it. After all, he'd been there for me first. "I'll go outside and get some fresh air."

"Stay close, please, and make sure the guards are in sight," Griffin said. He kissed my cheek and released my hand. "There've been enough attempts on your life to last a lifetime."

That was a very true statement. "I don't plan on venturing far." Not wanting to affect their conversation, I slipped out the back door and made my way around to the side of the house near the living room. They still had no idea how strong my hearing was, and I couldn't help but want to listen to what they had to say.

"Do you realize how important she is to me?" Killian asked. "If you ever hurt her—"

"I couldn't. It's not possible." Griffin sounded so sincere. "The connection is real. I swear it is."

Hope blossomed in my stomach. The scary truth was that I was at the mercy of our connection. I had no clue how powerfully the bond would impact us, but the more time I spent with him, the harder it was to leave his side. Each kiss and touch made the *tug* so much stronger.

"Oh, I believe that you think that." Killian sighed. "That's the only reason why your ass hasn't been beaten to a bloody pulp."

A smile slipped into place, and I made my way toward the wood's edge, not wanting to hear any more. They were coming to an agreement, and Killian hadn't wanted me to listen.

I focused on the sounds of the animals in the forest and glanced at the sun. It was midday when the sun was at its highest point in the sky and the moon farthest away, which meant I was at my weakest for the next few hours. At some point, I wanted to be able to shift and run free.

A *crack* sounded about a mile away and I jerked to a halt. Was that a gunshot? I scanned the area, realizing that the guards weren't in position. I'd been so caught up with Killian and Griffin that I hadn't been paying attention.

The noise took me back to the day when my pack had been murdered. I scanned the area, looking for one of the guards to alert, but I couldn't find one.

That was odd. They were supposed to be surrounding the house.

Another shot echoed, this one closer, followed by a low grunt.

Somebody was in trouble. I started to run in the direction of the shot, but I stopped. I couldn't leave Killian and Griffin and run off on my own. They'd be pissed, and rightfully so.

I rushed to the back door and threw it open. "Someone is in trouble, and the guards have disappeared." I stuck my head in to find them running toward the kitchen. Good, they were moving. "Call for backup. I'm going to go see what I can do."

"No," Griffin said absolutely. "You're staying here. It could be a trap."

Oh, hell no. "I may be attracted to you, but that doesn't mean I'll hand over my decision-making to you. I *am* going out there. It's up to you whether you come along for the ride."

A scream pierced the air, urging me back outside.

"Dove!" Griffin yelled as his footsteps pounded behind me. "Stop. We need to wait for backup."

"They can find us by following the noise." I spun around to face him. "We'll do recon first. We need to see what we're up against."

Killian stepped out of the house. "More of my guards are on their way."

"So are Shadow City guards," Griffin said.

"Great, let's go." I took off again and heard Griffin grumble something, though I couldn't make out the words.

Dad had taught me never to go on a mission without at least one other person knowing where I was headed.

I pulled magic from my wolf and picked up my pace with the guys on my heels as the trees flew by. We were headed in the direction of Killian's fishing spot from that day not too long ago.

When I crossed a path that appeared to have been made recently, the scent of the guards hit my nose, along with at least six others. Judging by how the branches were broken and scattered, someone had been dragged to wherever they went. Had someone gotten the jump on the guards?

It had to be the same assholes who'd attacked my pack.

The surrounding area was creepily quiet now that we'd stumbled across the trail. I slowed and lifted my hand, pivoting toward the two men. I placed a finger to my lips and gestured at the worn path.

Killian nodded as he walked over and touched the grass where it'd been flattened. I squatted next to him and held up four fingers, one for each guard. How the hell did they take the four guys?

"What—" Griffin started to ask quietly, but I covered his mouth with my hand. There was no telling how close anyone was.

This would have been when a pack bond would have come in handy.

"Come on out, Sterlyn," the voice of the auburn-bearded man called to me. He must have been at least a half-mile away, but I could hear him clear as day. "Or should I say Dove? We know you and those two guys that are always sniffing around you aren't far away."

Great, these assholes knew my names.

For them to know we were here meant someone was either listening for our progress or watching us. I tapped into my wolf more and scanned the area with precision. That was when I noticed a crow sitting on a tree branch not too far away. I sniffed the air, looking for a human smell mixed in with the vanilla of the animal.

When the bird flapped its wings and cawed, that confirmed all I needed to know. He was gloating, knowing we'd overlooked him.

Dammit. Crow shifters normally flocked in small groups and stayed out of matters unless it benefited them. What in the world were my hunters offering all of these different kinds of shifters to get them to work for them? They must have some incredibly enticing plan to get others to follow across races.

Another piece to the ever-growing puzzle.

There was no point in pretending that we weren't there. "How do you know my name?"

"What are you doing?" Killian whispered. "And when did you plan on telling me your name?"

"That crow—" I pointed to it "—already spotted us and reported back to Auburn Goatee." There was no point in pretending that we could do recon now. We were all-in, and I hoped the new guards would follow us soon. "And I was going to but got a little distracted."

Paws padded in our direction, and I assumed wolves were circling to trap us. The best thing we could do was try to get them talking. We needed to buy time for backup to find us. If we ran, they might take us down before the others could reach us.

"Please, come and join us." Goatee chuckled, no doubt loving that he had the upper hand.

"I'll come if you let the other two go." If I could protect Griffin and Killian, I would.

"Like hell." Griffin took my hand and shook his head. "There's no way I'll leave you."

Killian arched an eyebrow, and his mouth dropped slightly before he schooled his expression into one of indifference. "I'm with him. We aren't leaving."

"You need to go. They want me—you can't help me if they capture all of us." If I lost them, I wasn't sure I could stay in my right mind. "You two are alphas, for God's sake. You have to stay safe for your packs."

"Stop bickering," Goatee commanded. "They aren't going anywhere, and they aren't shifting. "

Four wolves stepped through two trees and circled us. The one right behind us growled and nodded his head forward, his milky brown fur blowing in the slight breeze.

Great, they were herding us to Goatee.

We started walking, slowly, Killian and Griffin flanking me as if they could protect me better than I could protect myself. They should be linking with their packs, pulling more guards toward us. But it could take time before they got here. I didn't know what skills either had, but I'd guess Killian might have been trained to fight similarly to me, given he was the alpha's son of the protecting pack. Griffin hadn't seemed to have formal training, but he was strong.

The river grew louder, and after a few more minutes, the trees grew thinner as we neared the embankment, close to the spot where Killian liked to fish. The four guards and Lucas lay dead on the mulchy ground, bullet holes between their eyes.

The present-day picture merged with the memory of my pack, and my legs grew shaky.

CHAPTER TWENTY

"What's wrong?" Goatee chuckled darkly. "Does this remind you of something?"

The asshole was gloating. He knew exactly what this was doing to me. That was probably why he'd had these five guards slaughtered this way. He wanted to break me and flaunt what they'd done to my pack. He had no remorse. "You had twenty guards on these five guards. From my standpoint, it was a small-dick move like the guns you used on my pack."

"Instead of insulting me, you should be thanking me. After all, we didn't kill you or your two boyfriends." Goatee *tsk*ed. "And these five deaths, well, they're on you."

"How so?" I wanted to understand his delusional justification. The next thing he would tell me was that I was to blame for my pack's death too, but I wasn't some weak-minded wolf. None of this was my fault, and I wouldn't let some self-absorbed asshole tell me otherwise.

"Because you ran away." The guy sneered and took a few steps in my direction. "Do you know how damn hard it was to find you?"

Killian and Griffin moved in front of me as if they could actually protect me. A laugh almost bubbled out of me, mainly due to what I'd seen of Griffin's fighting skills. I would need to train him if we did make it out of here alive.

Here I was, doubting myself. I had to believe that we would come out of this breathing, all three of us, or I might as well lie down and give up. But we needed backup, so I had to stall.

"I'm pretty sure you found me that second day." That had to have been him exiting the diner that morning when I had my meltdown. "Granted, you made me doubt it when you walked off without a second glance."

"We had been at a loss until that moment." Goatee scowled. "We actually were passing through the city and didn't think you'd run here of all places with the number of people here that could identify a silver wolf. It was a good strategy, but this was obviously fate. By the way, what did you think of the little calling-card we left for you?"

Of course. That explains seeing the wolf right after I found the painting on the wall. "Fuck you," I spat.

"Gladly," Auburn Goatee chuckled. "But we can get to that part as soon as we get you settled in your new home."

My skin crawled at the insinuation.

"She is *not* yours," Griffin said with menace. "She's mine, and you won't be taking her anywhere."

"You have no influence over me, alpha boy." Goatee rubbed his hands together and gestured to the five dead guards.

"If you hurt Sterlyn or injure another one of my people, you will have made an enemy out of Shadow City." Griffin straightened his shoulders, standing tall. "If you stand down now, we can come to an agreement. I have the power to protect you from the punishment you deserve and *will* receive if you try to take Sterlyn or harm any of us. Tell us what you're looking for. Entry to Shadow City? A place in a new pack?"

"Oh, no." Goatee placed a hand over his mouth and forced his body to shake. "What ever shall I do?" He glanced over his shoulder as ten more men slipped through the trees behind him and joined us. "We have no other choice than to leave right now. After all, the big powerful Shadow City alpha might not like us. Oh, wait. He already doesn't, and Shadow City only lets in wolves that can benefit them. So I guess that means I don't give two fucks about negotiating with you."

A few of his men chuckled, clearly enjoying watching the alpha wolf of the elusive city being made fun of.

Griffin had to see that this group of idiots wasn't afraid of consequences. Either their own alpha had commanded them to retrieve me, or they were getting paid big bucks. There was no negotiating with them because they didn't work in diplomatic ways, so I'd cut straight to the chase. "I'm not going with you. I refuse to be some dickwad's personal breeder."

A low growl escaped Griffin. "You'll have to kill me to take her."

The fact that they hadn't killed Griffin both worried and relieved me. They obviously didn't want him dead, but why? There had to be more going on than we even guessed originally.

"We can arrange that," Goatee cooed. "Or we can walk away here as friends, and you get over your little-boy crush. Either way, she'll be coming with us."

"My sister isn't going to be some guy's sex slave," Killian said. "Griffin is right; you'll have to kill both of us."

I couldn't let them sacrifice themselves for me. That

would be something I couldn't live with. "If you don't hurt them, I'll willingly go with you." The fact that they hadn't yet hurt or killed either guy made me think there was a reason, that maybe they had orders not to. If I went willingly and played the part for a while, they'd possibly let Killian and Griffin go, and I could determine a way to escape. It would no doubt be hard, but under the moon, I might be able to swing it.

"No." Griffin shook his head. "You aren't going with them. Absolutely not." He clenched his hands into fists, and some honey brown fur sprouted across his arms. He was dangerously close to shifting.

The time still wasn't right to start the fight. I couldn't hear any additional guards running in our direction. And that stupid crow would probably know they were coming long before we did, what with being perched on that damn tall tree not ten yards away.

"See, this is why I tried to leave last night." If I got Griffin to focus on me, that should hold him back. "I didn't want you and Killian to get hurt foolishly for me."

"Well, then, a thank you is in order." Goatee rubbed his hands together. "She would've gotten the slip on us since I was gathering the troops after confirming it was her at the university yesterday."

Of course, he'd done the drawing and watched me make an ass of myself with Rosemary. The memory of the wolf in the woods triggered—he'd been in the shadows, and I hadn't noticed that his fur had a red hue to it, but thinking back, it was pretty damn clear.

The crow flew off the branch, crying, "Caw! Caw! Caw!"

That was when the noise of multiple feet pounded on the ground, heading in our direction.

"They have backup." One of the lanky guys in the back called as he stood, pulling out a machine gun.

Dear, sweet Jesus. This wasn't going to end well, and not enough guards were heading this way. Maybe more were coming, but Goatee's men would try to pick them off one at a time, which meant a fight was inevitable. We'd have to distract as many as possible so the guards wouldn't end up like these other five.

Doing the only thing I could think of in this moment, I called my wolf forward. I had no weapon because I foolishly hadn't planned to come outside, so my animal was the only option I had.

I was born for battle. I had to trust my instincts.

My skin tingled as my silver fur sprouted all over my body, and my bones cracked, contorting me to my animal form. My clothes ripped away as my four paws hit the ground.

"Dammit, she shifted." The scrawny shifter swung the gun in my direction. "What do we do?" His voice held a slight tremor.

Good, at least, they weren't comfortable with me.

Goatee spun around and knocked the gun away from my direction. "You do not shoot her unless there is absolutely no other choice. Got it? If we don't get her there alive, you'll be taking the blame."

That little bit of information was music to my ears. They didn't want to kill me, which meant I had a little leeway before they'd be willing to do it.

Deciding to use their distraction to my advantage, I ran through Killian and Griffin and locked on the scrawny guy who'd been foolish enough to show weakness. That would make the others pause around me.

What I wanted was to attack Goatee, but he was in control of this little pack, which meant I had to be smart.

A few of the men froze as I ran past them. It was clear that they'd never been around a silver wolf in wolf form before. Since we were close to a full moon, I was larger than all of them. My pack called a full moon a silver moon, in celebration of the strength of our connection.

Killian and Griffin followed my lead and shifted behind me while the others stayed focused on me. I hated that they were here with me, but I knew they wouldn't leave.

Even though time seemed to move slowly, only a few seconds had passed. I lunged at the lanky guy and sank my teeth into his neck, jerked my head to the side, and killed him on the spot. Blood dripped down my mouth, covering my fur as the taste of copper stuck to my tongue and the metallic scent hit my nose.

My stomach churned. I hated death and being the one to cause it, but I had to hold it together. It was us or them, and there were twenty-three enemies in human form, four wolves, and a crow to go. I'd seen what they were capable of and refused to let anyone else I loved die because of a moment's hesitation.

Dad had told me that we should never celebrate killing others and do it only when absolutely necessary.

I'd challenged him, asking how you would know whether it was necessary or not. And he'd patted my arm and replied that I would know. That our wolves would guide us because they were good and thus made of pure light as well. That we were a reflection of the power inside us.

I never believed him until now, but there was no question in my mind that these assholes had to die. They got off on hurting others and asserting their dominance, and I refused to let the cycle continue. The cost of their sins was their lives.

"What are you standing around for?" Goatee yelled. "Attack to incapacitate. Don't kill the girl."

Dark fur rushed past me as Killian went into battle mode. He jumped on one of the closer men, sinking his teeth into the arm that had been going for his gun.

Killian made decisions like a fighter, so that was one less person to worry about.

An arm wrapped around my neck, cutting off some of my oxygen. The man who had me jerked me upright, pulling me up to my hind legs. I turned my head, trying to bite some part of his arm, but the enemy had me in an iron-clad hold. I dug my front claws into his arm, which made him groan. But no matter how deep I dug into his skin, his hold didn't slacken.

"You're not getting out that easily," the guy cackled. "You aren't the only one who knows how to fight."

I loved having an arrogant opponent. There was nothing quite as motivating as proving their asses wrong and watching them squirm when they realized they were outmatched.

The enemy chuckled as if he'd gotten the upper hand. That was my cue to push backward and let my entire weight fall on his chest. He wasn't prepared for it, so he fell on his back with me right on top. I rolled off him quickly and stood on him.

His soulless eyes widened as he realized I'd outsmarted him. Not giving him a chance to react, I clawed his neck deep, letting the blood pour to the ground. At least, I didn't have to taste it this time.

I glanced in Griffin's direction and almost cried in relief when I realized he was holding his own against three guards. His wolf was very strong and knew what to do. So fighting was a weakness only in his human form. I could work with that.

A guard squatting between two trees five feet away lifted his gun in Griffin's direction. My wolf howled, and we ran with blinding speed toward the guy as his finger tightened on the trigger. I lowered my head and rammed it between his legs, lifting him up like he was riding a bull.

He fell forward as the gun fired, and the bullet missed its mark—short by three feet, and the guy landed on his face.

A rustling forced my attention back to Goatee. He loaded some kind of tranquilizer dart into a gun and pointed it at me. "This has gone on far to long."

Shit. I had to time my movement, or my fight would be over. I inched toward a tree, as he aimed right at me.

Taking a deep breathe, I tried to remain calm and act scared, like I'd given up. I lowered my head, but not enough that I couldn't see what he was doing. His finger pulled the trigger, and I channeled every ounce of speed into racing behind the tree.

The breeze of the dart hit my tail as I narrowly escaped impact.

"Fuck!" Goatee screamed as his face turned red. "The tranq missed the mark, so all of you need to get your asses in gear."

Goatee charged Killian, who was fighting off a man with a knife.

It was clear these were all shifters who more comfortable using their weapons than their animals, which boded well for us in a way. No matter how bad things got, they would shift only if that was their last option.

My animal knew that Goatee was trying to trick me. She took note that he wasn't moving as fast as he could, and he had his head turned slightly in my direction as if waiting for me to charge. All of that told me he had no intention of attacking Killian.

I couldn't let him know that I was on to his plan. I rushed toward him like he was expecting, but as I reached him, I spun out of the way.

He turned on his heel and swung a knife where my shoulder would've been. However, all he did was hit air as he turned in a complete circle, expecting an impact. He sneered at me as his breathing increased.

"You stupid bitch," he growled. "You won't get away this time, no matter what kind of game you try to play."

Game? That was what he called this? This *game* was not only about the fact that my life was at risk, but it involved the lives of the two people left that I cared dearly for. I risked losing everything. *This* was about survival.

I hunkered down and bared my teeth at him. Our guards were getting closer, at least, giving us some more backup. I glanced around and noted that all four wolves and eight enemy shifters were now missing, probably gone to stop our guards. I hated that the guards were being ambushed, but for the moment, that helped Killian, Griffin, and me. With Killian and Griffin pack linking with the guards, they should be somewhat prepared for what they were walking into.

Gunshots fired, and a sharp pain pierced my hind leg. I staggered back a few steps, trying to keep my balance, but placing weight on the injured leg caused me to collapse.

The sharp pain morphed into fire as if my leg were being burned. I turned to find blood trickling down my silver fur.

I'd been shot.

"We tried to do it the nice way." Goatee squatted beside me and held his knife in front of my face. "But you wouldn't have that. So you're forcing our hand... again."

My heart hammered. Maybe they didn't have to bring me in alive after all.

CHAPTER TWENTY-ONE

My focus locked on the knife Goatee wielded in my face as my training kicked in. This guy was insane, and there was a glint in his eyes, informing me he loved the hold he had on me. He placed the knife against my throat, letting it cut through my fur and slice my skin.

My skin burned, but that was the wake-up call I needed. He would hurt me little by little, which would lead to me losing my mind.

Fear could paralyze and make someone irrational, which meant if I didn't get a hold of myself, I would be playing right into his hands.

I refused to do that.

To make it easier for him.

I had to make them pay for what they'd done. Being smarter than them shouldn't have been hard. They relied on terror, weapons, and surprise attacks.

In my peripheral vision, I could see both Killian and Griffin holding their own, but we were each fighting multiple enemies. Goatee's men outnumbered us by eleven, and the enemies were attacking Griffin and Killian in groups of five while four were locked on me. But that was both good and bad. Good because they thought we'd have backup imminently, so they wanted to end the fight quickly, and bad because they'd do whatever it took to end it as quickly as possible.

Goatee had to be my first priority. I needed to get out of his clutches to help my guys and the other guards who were on their way.

The other three men on me circled, watching their leader subdue me. Or so they thought.

"Don't worry." Goatee leaned forward like he was telling me a secret. "They won't see us take you. We'll knock them out before we drag you away. And we *will* kill them if we have to—if you don't cooperate."

Like hell that would ever happen. I refused to be a puppet in this sick game. But that was the problem. I had no damn clue what game they were playing, which put us at a disadvantage. Who was the man behind all of this who desperately wanted me as his own?

The knife slackened against my neck as Goatee turned his head to watch what was going on with Griffin and Killian.

This was the distraction I needed. Going with pure instinct, I clamped down on the wrist of Goatee's hand that was holding the knife until my teeth hit the bone. This was my opportunity to even out the fight.

He hissed as his blood dripped down my chin, mixing with that of the lanky guy I'd killed only minutes earlier and my own blood where Goatee had cut me. My mouth tensed as I waited for him to yank in desperation to free his hand, but his face only contorted into rage.

Shit. I'd miscalculated. Maybe he had some brains after all.

His free arm moved toward my body as he aimed for my bullet wound, but since I was in wolf form, I was a little faster.

I released my hold on him and rolled out of the way as his hand only skimmed my fur. I stood on all fours, placing most of my weight on the three uninjured legs.

The three other men began to move toward me, but Goatee yelled, "Stop! This bitch is mine."

He wanted to make a statement, not only with me but with his men too. He could take down a silver wolf all by himself.

"You got lucky." Goatee clutched his injured hand close to his body as he bent down and grabbed the knife. "But don't worry. I can use my left hand just as well."

I had a feeling he wasn't bluffing, which meant I had to injure that hand too.

Game on.

I snarled, wanting him to know that he didn't scare me. We were on even ground, even though I didn't like to admit that my hind leg was as much of a strategic liability as his injured hand.

He swung his knife at me, making it clear that he wasn't scared. This wasn't only a battle of skill but of proving something to each other.

Breaking me was his end goal, whereas mine was proving that he couldn't.

I stumbled back, avoiding the blow, but that had been his real intent. I placed more weight than I could handle on my back leg and almost fell.

Goatee scowled when I managed to stay on all four legs.

My silver wolf healing abilities worked faster than other wolves, which worked in my favor. My leg still hurt like a son of a bitch, but I could already feel it knitting together and was able to put more weight on it. Unfortunately, the bullet was still lodged inside, which meant that I'd have to reopen the wound to get it out, but that was yet another problem for later.

Needing to strike first, I charged his right side. He would be weakest there and not able to counter as well. Before I connected with him, I noticed a tree with a low-hanging branch a few feet away and changed my plan mid-stride. At this point, I didn't care about making him suffer, I only wanted this entire thing over so I could help the others.

I lowered my head and bulldozed him into the branch. The sound of ripping skin and a groan of pain told me that I'd hit the mark. I took a few steps back and saw the end of the branch sticking through his shoulder. My intent had been to skewer his heart, but at least, he was worse off than me now. Even though the wound seemed to have missed the main artery, there was so much blood his subclavian may have been nicked.

"Attack her!" Goatee demanded. "She can't get away. As long as she can survive, do whatever is necessary to make her leave with us. Take them down and kill them if she doesn't yield."

The three enemy guards sprang into action like they'd been waiting for this moment. Additionally, one guard from both Killian and Griffin spun in my direction with hunger in their own eyes. Each one wanted to have a claim on taking down the almost extinct silver wolf line. At least, that helped both Griffin and Killian with their own battles.

One pointed his gun at the side of my body that wasn't injured. They were going to try to weaken both sides.

Shit, I didn't know how to get out of this. I scanned the woods desperately for an idea, but there wasn't a damn thing I could think of. My best bet was to run and make them chase me. It might hurt like hell, but as long as I survived, that was okay.

I took off running toward the water as more gunfire echoed farther away from where Griffin's and Killian's additional guards were coming in.

Someone fired at me, missing by mere inches. The bullet lodged in the dirt, making it splatter.

I had to run faster.

Trees blurred by as I pushed harder. With each step, my leg grew a little stronger, which was a blessing in this hellish situation.

When an opening between two trees came into view, I made a sharp left, planning to double back to where Killian and Griffin were. The five men chasing me were falling behind.

As I rushed toward Griffin and Killian, one of the enemies yelled, "I'm going to shift. Otherwise, she'll outrun us."

Even though that sucked, at least, it would be one less person with a gun or knife.

When I broke through the clearing, an enemy had a gun to Killian's head while two others were laughing despite one of their own being dead at their feet. It was as if their friend's life had meant nothing.

My world wanted to stop, but I pushed through the mental block, racing toward the enemy. I growled low and threatening, making him pause and glance in my direction. His mouth dropped in shock like he hadn't expected to see me, and the other two stumbled back a few feet.

They weren't so cocky when they were the ones being surprised.

That was the distraction Killian needed in order to spin around and pounce on his attacker. The man screamed in agony as Killian ripped him apart while his two friends stood there and watched the gruesome attack with open mouths.

My heart hurt to see so much death and destruction, but this was the cruel necessity of war. I blew past Killian, heading toward Griffin and the others. We had to level the odds as fast as possible. The longer they outnumbered us, the more deaths there would be on our end.

Three feet away, Griffin was fighting two men who had knives instead of guns. He'd managed to take down two during my run, which meant our numbers were getting more favorable by the minute.

Gunshots were still firing not too far away. The fact that the enemy fighters hadn't returned meant that Killian's and Griffin's guards weren't being decimated as I feared.

My eyes flicked to where Goatee had been to find him gone. The branch remained covered in his blood and pieces of muscle and skin. The bastard had been determined to get free, I had to give him that.

But right then, I needed to help Griffin. I struck at the enemy nearest me, biting into his leg. The guy screamed as he turned his attention to me. He swung his knife toward my side, but Griffin attacked, sinking his teeth into the guy's jugular. The man's eyes widened as he dropped the knife and grasped his throat as if that was going to prevent the fatality of his injury.

The other man used our distraction to pick up his friend's discarded knife. I released my hold, allowing Griffin to finish the job, and turned my attention to the uninjured guy, taking advantage of the angle and biting deep into his side. The wound reminded me of the one they'd given my father.

Poetic justice.

Griffin sniffed me over, focusing on my wound. His hazel eyes filled with concern as he nuzzled his head against me. His closeness centered me, bringing me back from the horrible memory. The comforting *tug* of our connection made me feel whole.

"Aw, how cute. You think you might actually win, but my men and I have been holding back." Goatee croaked and waved to his men to come toward him as he stepped into view along with the remaining four men in human form and the lone wolf. "But this is over." Blood trickled down his shirt, soaking it.

Killian growled and stepped in front of me, sides heaving. Griffin flanked my injured side, baring his teeth through the blood coating his muzzle. Those two were showing that they would protect me no matter the cost.

The two men that had been fighting Killian joined Goatee as they regrouped and stared us down. Each one tensed and poised, waiting for their instructions.

"Fuck the orders. Kill them." Goatee glanced down at his fatal wound, and his nostrils flared. Pure hatred reflected as he locked eyes with me. "I want her to watch them die."

At this moment, there were seven of them and only one wolf against our three. At the rate we were going, we could have kept chipping away at their numbers as long as we continued to hold on. But we'd foolishly given them time to regroup, and they circled us with weapons.

I shook my head no. I would do anything to be sure Griffin and Killian lived. At least, they would have a chance at happiness, and I'd figure out a way to escape. It might take days or months, but eventually, these people would let down their guard.

"No?" Goatee walked to me and grabbed my snout. "You going to behave then?"

Griffin growled as he inched toward the prick.

"Don't come another step closer or you'll regret it," Goatee threatened.

Griffin ignored him, but I bumped him away.

"I tried to warn you." Goatee sighed as he wrapped his uninjured hand around my leg, jabbing a finger into the healing bullet hole.

Intense pain coursed through my body, and even in animal form, my stomach revolted from the intensity. A whimper wanted to escape, but I clamped it down, refusing to show weakness.

"I gotta say, I do enjoy that you force me to do these things." Goatee smirked as the engine of a boat purred toward us. "You gave me a plausible excuse for my alpha when he demands to know why I had to do this to you."

Dammit, the getaway vehicle was on its way. If we didn't figure out something fast, then I'd be going with them.

Goatee dug his finger deeper into my wound, determined to make me cry out. He wanted these two guys to hear my pain. He was messing with me, trying to make me believe that they might get out alive if I cooperated.

Gathering all of my strength, I pushed back the pain and focused. That was when I realized that he'd actually opened himself up to an attack. He'd been banking on me being too overcome with pain to try to attack him.

Arrogance was a blessing.

I bit into the shoulder of the arm he had wrapped around me and shredded his skin, biting as deep as possible. This time, he couldn't ignore it, and his hand slipped out of my wound as he yelled and jerked forward, trying to stick the bloody finger into my eye.

"Jimmy," one of his men called out. "What do we do?"

Their uncertainty fueled my adrenaline, and I bulldozed him over onto his back, knocking the breath out of him.

A loud howl hurt my ears as I watched Griffin attack one of the enemies who was holding a gun. The weapon fell, and when the guy reached down to get it, Griffin lunged, slashing his teeth through the back of the guy's neck with a sickening cracking noise. The guy crumbled.

Goatee used my distraction against me as his finger connected with my eye. As the pressure increased, my heart sank, and I realized that I could lose my eye.

Killian attacked another man with a gun while Griffin ran toward me.

I hated that he was running to me instead of attacking the other guard, but right now, I was at a huge disadvantage, and the guard seemed confused as to whether he should help Goatee or fight Griffin.

The boat motor grew louder, and the pungent smell of gas wafted around us. It was that damn close.

"Shoot her other leg before she kills me." Goatee cried as his voice began to slur from blood loss. His finger's pressure reduced on my eye as his strength finally began to fade. "Now!"

The gun clicked as it was cocked, and I braced for the pain. I only hoped that the guy missed his mark and killed me.

Death would be more welcome than living through whatever they planned to do to me.

A loud, heartbreaking howl pummeled my ears as Griffin jumped in front of me.

No, what was he doing? The guy was going to shoot!

As the gun fired, I jerked away from Goatee, desperate to get Griffin out of the way. Considering the angle at which the enemy guard was trying to shoot me and the way

Griffin landed in front of me, it would be a kill shot for him.

But my legs fell out from under me, and Griffin's wolfish body took the bullet in his chest. The momentum knocked him backward, and he fell hard next to my legs.

CHAPTER TWENTY-TWO

This had to be some crazy dream. A horrible nightmare that I could wake from. I couldn't have lost Griffin before we even had a chance to embrace our relationship.

Watching him bleed out forced me to realize my biggest regret.

Being too scared to bond with him.

A loud howl vibrated all around us, and it took a moment to realize that the cry was coming from me. My heartbreak shattered my soul, and hatred flowed through my body.

I'd be damned if I left with these assholes. After everything they'd taken away from me, I'd rather die than give them what they wanted.

The thrumming of the boat engine indicated it was almost upon us. We were running out of time, no one more than Griffin.

"Ssseee," Goatee slurred, barely able to keep his eyes open. "We will always wiiinnnn."

Not if I have anything to do with it.

Anger fueled my body, and I gathered enough resolve to

put weight on my front paws and reach his neck to rip out his throat. For the first time ever, I didn't feel remorse. Numbness took over.

Large black wings rushed past me, helping rage ward off the strange haze I was locked in.

That damn bird topped my shit list, seeing as he'd probably been watching me for longer than I'd ever realized. I'd pluck him feather by feather until he couldn't handle it and turned back to his human form.

I turned to attack before the crow could hurt Griffin more but stopped short when my gaze landed on Rosemary instead. All of the enemy guards lay dead on the ground except two. One was engaged in battle with Killian while the other swung his gun in the dark wolf's direction, ready to shoot.

No. I can't lose him too.

I tried to stand on both legs but fell hard on my stomach. Whether I wanted to admit it or not, Goatee had done a number on me. All I could do was lie there in agony as the last man got ready to shoot Killian.

As the gun fired, Rosemary circled her wings, making her feathers blend together and surround her. She stepped between the bullet and Killian.

Did she have a death wish? I watched in horror as the bullet hit her...and bounced off her wings.

"What the—" the guy stuttered as he dropped his gun.

She unfolded her wings, a smirk on her face. "Angels are hard to kill." She jumped, flying directly at him, and the guy had enough sense to turn and run.

The idiot ran in the direction of the boat, like that would protect him.

Before he could escape from view, Rosemary caught up and grabbed him around the neck. A loud *crack* followed, and his body smacked to the ground, clearly dead on impact.

Thank God she was here because Killian would have been dead if she hadn't arrived.

Killian.

I turned to find his dark fur soaked with blood, but the last enemy lay dead at his feet. For the moment, we were safe, so I crawled toward Griffin and laid my head next to his. I whimpered as both my wolf and I mourned the man beside me.

He brushed his head against mine and nuzzled my face.

This was wrong. We couldn't even communicate in this form. I couldn't tell him my regrets or how I wished things had gone differently. All I could do was lie beside him as he died.

"I need you to move," Rosemary said as she squatted on Griffin's other side. She reached her hands toward him, and I growled.

No one but me could touch him right now. I needed to be the one he was with when he transitioned out.

Rosemary arched a brow and tilted her head. "Did you growl at me?"

I bared my teeth, emphasizing my point. My wolf surged forward. I wasn't sure how much clearer I could get.

"Do you want me to save him or not?" She bobbed her head as she tapped her fingers on her jeans. "Once he's dead, I can't bring him back."

I lifted my head and stared at her. She could save him? Was this some sort of joke? I looked at Killian, wanting him to give me a sign.

He nodded, alleviating some of my concern.

Griffin's breathing began to slow, and his eyelids fluttered close. He was fading, and I had to put his life before my own possessive tendencies.

Everything inside me screamed for me to not allow her to touch him, but I reined in my animal. Of course, being injured made it more difficult for me. If she did do something to him, I wouldn't be able to protect him, and that made me more volatile.

"I'm going to try again." Rosemary narrowed her eyes at me. "And if you bite me, this will be the last time I help you."

She might not be the nicest person in the world, but she was blunt, and I knew where she stood. I did respect her for that. Not many people were that forthcoming. I scooted away, letting her know that I wouldn't be a problem.

"Good girl," she chuckled.

Great, she'd already gotten cocky enough for dog jokes, but if that was what it took to save Griffin, I'd gladly take them.

She placed one hand on Griffin's wound and the other on my hip. Her skin began to glow.

White light poured from her fingers, and a warm buzzing sensation smacked me straight in the chest—a fluttering feeling of safety and security like everything would be okay. It reminded me of when I was a little girl and my mom would hold me in her arms.

Rosemary's stardust irises glowed a brilliant white as her power charged all around us. If I'd thought she was breathtaking before, I was wrong. Now she was transcendent.

I watched in awe as Griffin's chest rose once again. After a long moment, Rosemary's skin began to fade into her normal pale complexion. She dropped her hands and faced me. "Your leg should be better also."

That was why I'd felt so safe. She'd healed both Griffin and me at the same time. I'd heard that angels were powerful beings, but that was downplaying their abilities.

Griffin slowly sat up on his hind legs, and the relief that burst through my heart was jarring. I jumped on him, forcing him to his back. I was so damn happy that he was okay. He licked my face as he rolled over on top of me, his tongue hanging out of his mouth.

"As much as I hate to interrupt your play, your guards are still under attack, and a boat pulled up to wait for these idiots to get away." Rosemary stood and brushed the dirt off her jeans.

She was right. We needed to help the others. There wasn't as much gunfire, but no one had made it to us. Our new priority was protecting Killian's and Griffin's packs.

I jerked my head in the direction where the others should be and took off running. There was absolutely no pain in my leg, which surprised me. Rosemary had been able to heal my leg completely, even removing the bullet.

The only question was: Why had she helped us? In general, people didn't go into battle willingly for anyone who wasn't a friend or an ally. Even though we weren't enemies, our interactions hadn't been the best. She must have a reason for helping. Yet another issue to deal with later.

Rosemary flapped her wings, ascending into the sky. "I'll meet you there." She flew in the opposite direction faster than my four legs could take me.

As we followed our trail back toward the guards, the sound of fighting grew louder. I wasn't sure if I should be relieved or not, but at least, some of their guards had to still be standing.

The crow fluttered into the sky again, cawing over and

over, letting the enemy guards know that we were approaching.

Forcing myself not to waste any more negative energy on that stupid thing, I scanned the area, taking in the damage. There were bodies littered everywhere.

This whole attack was eerily similar to the one back home. Maybe I should've gone with Goatee and kept all these people safe.

Killian took the lead, racing toward a wolf who was surrounded by three others. He growled loudly, drawing the attention of the enemies from their target.

I followed Killian's lead with Griffin running beside me. The attackers didn't outnumber the lone surviving guard any longer. In fact, they were now the ones who were outmatched.

Running to the side, I targeted the large milky brown wolf who'd been with Goatee earlier. The cruel glint in his eye matched the abyss deep inside him, revealing a sickness even worse than Goatee's. Maybe Goatee wasn't the one I should've been most focused on. Discovering two souls so full of hatred made me even more worried about whomever they were working under.

At least, I could get rid of one more jerkwad.

He faced me in a clear challenge. He knew who I was and sneered at me with determination, examining me, waiting to predict my next move. He was probably the most skilled fighter of his group.

Not wanting to give away my plan, I slowed as if I had nothing to prove. Technically, I didn't, but I did want to survive.

Killian and Griffin attacked two of the wolves as I sat in front of the larger one, pretending I wasn't fazed in the least. We were in a standoff. He wanted to see what he was up against while I wanted to see what strategy he'd use.

The best way to piss off a man who was trying to prove himself was to belittle him. I forced my shoulders to shake and made the choking bark sound of a wolf laughing.

He snorted and shook his head, giving me a sign that I was getting under his skin. His quickened panting let me know that his anger was beginning to get the best of him.

I glanced at Griffin and Killian, making sure they were doing okay but also to indicate that I wasn't fazed by the increasingly angry wolf watching me. Even though I could see him in my peripheral vision, not paying attention to him was the final straw.

Inching toward me, he kept his eyes locked on my face. I pretended to not notice his approach, despite my entire focus now being on him since Griffin and Killian were holding their own.

With each stride toward me, he grew bolder and angrier when I didn't bat an eyelash. His body grew rigid, and I knew he would attack at any moment. How he charged me would tell me the most about him.

Now only ten feet away, he growled, wanting me to acknowledge he was there. When I turned my head his way, he lunged.

Brute force. That was his plan, which was what I'd suspected.

I rolled out of the way as he landed on all four legs where I'd been. He snarled and pivoted, teeth bared, drool dripping down his chin. He reminded me of a rabid dog.

Hell, he might have been truly rabid.

Not bothering to change strategy, he lunged at me once more, aiming for my shoulder. Like Goatee, he didn't want to kill me, just injure me severely. But he wasn't thinking it through because Killian and Griffin were here as well. Even if he took me down, how was he going to get himself and my injured body to the boat when they were both here?

The one surviving guard on our side barreled toward me. He was coming to help me fight this wolf.

Where I differed from this crazed wolf and Goatee was that I didn't have to prove myself. They enjoyed dominating others to get ahead, but real protectors fought to win, not to come out on top. Protecting was about doing what was best for everyone, pushing vanity and self-worth aside. There was no room for ego. I'd welcome the help as long as it stopped more innocents from dying.

The enemy wolf didn't even bother turning in the guard's direction. He was focused solely on me, which was both stupid and scary. How could someone have such a one-track mind when their death could be imminent?

But that was the thing; he didn't see anything outside of me.

The guard jumped on the milk chocolate wolf's back and stuck his claws into its side as his teeth sank into the spot between his neck and shoulder.

As if realizing the magnitude of his injuries, the enemy wolf stood on both hind legs, trying to fall back onto the guard so he would release his hold.

I refused to allow him the opportunity, I jumped forward and sank my teeth into the front of his neck, ready for this whole damn fight to be over. The guy's eyes widened, and I jerked my head hard, assuring he would die instantaneously.

At this point, I didn't care about them paying for their sins. I wanted the fight done.

With the weight of the guard on his back, the wolf landed on his face but was already dead before impact.

The world seemed to pause as I surveyed the area and realized that all of the enemy fighters were dead. But the heartbreaking fact was that Killian, Griffin, this one guard, and myself were the only survivors on our side. I had no clue how many of their pack had come to aid us and died.

A caw and the flutter of wings caught my attention as the crow flew high, away from the mess on the ground.

We had to catch him before he alerted whoever was behind this ambush.

CHAPTER TWENTY-THREE

Of course, the damn bird was flying back toward the boat, probably to alert the people on board that everyone was dead. There was no way we could beat him to it.

But dammit, we had to try. I howled and took off in the direction of the river once more, Griffin, Killian, and the guard right behind me.

I kept my eyes forward, refusing to glance at the bodies as I passed. So much death and destruction, and it was all because of me. If I'd gone willingly, would this have turned out differently?

I had to push those thoughts aside. Focus on the here and now.

Within seconds, I passed through the trees, and the river came into view. I stepped into puddles of what could only be blood, the metallic scent confirming my suspicions.

But I powered through.

The three wolves behind me panted, trying to keep up, but I couldn't slow. If I wanted to have a chance at catching the people on the boat, we had to get there fast.

A loud caw sounded again, closer than I expected. It was a call of fear and desperation. I glanced skyward only to see the crow fly over our heads back in the direction we'd come from.

What the hell would have caused that?

Large wings whooshed behind me, answering my question. I glanced over my shoulder, surprised to find Rosemary landing a few feet away.

Blood covered her arms, and the shoulder of her shirt was ripped. "The shifters on the boat are dead." She nodded in the direction of the water. "I figured I could take them out while the rest of you focused on saving your men and yourselves."

I couldn't speak to her in this form to tell her I was grateful. All I could do was nod.

Even though I hated that the bird got away, at least the boat hadn't managed to leave.

"Why don't you four go back and shift to human so you can get more help to clean up the bodies?" Rosemary said with authority. "I'll meet you at the house in a few minutes."

Normally, being told what to do would irritate me, but after the way she'd helped us and all of the fighting, shifting back and regrouping sounded nice. We needed to take care of our dead and figure out our next moves, but for the moment, we didn't have to worry about another attack.

I turned around and found Griffin waiting for me and Killian and the guard trotting off together, leaving the two of us to head back alone.

My heart warmed and welcomed the sensation of the *tug*. For a minute there, I thought I'd never have the chance to walk beside him again. I hurried to him, not wanting to stay out here another second.

STEPPING out of the shower was one of the hardest things I'd had to do. Between needing to wash the blood from my body, the deaths I had caused, and just being sore from not training as I should have, all I wanted to do was stay in the warm spray of water.

But that wasn't an option because of a certain dark angel pacing the living room.

"What the hell is taking her so long?" Rosemary complained. "When she said she was taking a shower, I didn't think I'd be stuck out here with you two idiots for this long."

"First off, this is my house," Killian growled. "And second, she's been in there five minutes. Give her a break."

Ugh, maybe I should turn the water back on. She seemed to be in a mood.

Granted, she was always kind of like this, so I shouldn't have been surprised. I quickly dried and got dressed.

"Do you know what I risked by helping you fight those wolves?" Rosemary's tone grew angry. "If that jackass Azbogah learns what I did, he'll give my parents hell. I risked a lot—"

Griffin's anger was palpable as he said, "The water has turned off, so you can slow down. No one asked you to help, so don't come in here, demanding certain things. If my mate—"

"Your *mate?*" Rosemary snorted. "Are you kidding me? This gets better and better."

"What's so funny about that?" Griffin rasped.

"You don't even want to be alpha, and now you're mated to a wolf like *her.*" She sighed. "Can you get any luckier?"

Inhaling sharply, I quickly dressed in the jeans and shirt

I'd worn the day when Killian found me. I'd been avoiding wearing these clothes, but after destroying the new ones, I didn't have much choice. I opened the door and strolled into the living room.

I straightened my shoulders and stared the angel down. "Thank you for fighting alongside us and helping, but you don't get to come in here and treat us like we're worthless." She and I had a very odd relationship, to say the least. I didn't dislike her, but she was abrasive and rash.

"See, that's why I like you." Rosemary turned her back on Killian and Griffin. "You get straight to the point without trying to prove you have a dick."

A smile broke through my face. "It's kind of hard to prove I have one when the appendage is missing."

"It makes things easier that way." Rosemary laughed.

"Uh... what's happening?" Killian asked Griffin.

"No clue, man." Griffin shook his head as he walked over to me and took my hand. "But her being nice is kind of freaking me out."

"And they wonder why I don't want to bother talking to them." She shook her head. "But I'm assuming they're kind of a package deal?"

"Yeah, they are." I stepped closer to Griffin, needing to feel him. "So how did you know we were in trouble?"

"I didn't." Rosemary strolled to the windows overlooking the pool and backyard. "I was actually on my way to find you about our little talk the other day."

My eyes flicked toward the tree line where several shifters were heading out back to take care of the dead. After we'd gotten back to the houses and shifted, more Shadow Ridge and Shadow City shifters had arrived. Luckily, I'd already gone inside, so none of them saw me in my silver wolf form. However, I needed to hurry and get out there to help them. After all, this carnage was all my fault. "Well, you found more than you bargained for."

"You do realize you need to tell Zac that he can't tell anyone about what she is." Rosemary scowled at Griffin. "The more people who realize she's a silver wolf, the more at risk she'll be."

"We've already handled that." Griffin stood tall beside me. "I commanded him with the alpha will. He can't tell anyone, not even his family."

Killian leaned against the wall on the other side of the window. "Not that he would've anyway."

"Don't be so certain." Rosemary rolled her shoulders. She looked at me. "But that's not why I'm here. Fortunately, if you can keep these two and the guard quiet, it appears no one else knows that a silver wolf has rejoined our society. At least, not on the angel side of things."

"That's good news, right?" The fewer people who knew about me, the safer we all would be.

"For now." Rosemary gestured to Griffin as she continued, "But if you two are fated mates, how long do you think your little secret can last?"

My heart sank. I hadn't even thought about that.

"I'll leave with her." Griffin made it sound so simple.

I jerked my head toward him. "You can't do that." Especially if what Rosemary had said about a civil war brewing was true. "You are their leader. Fate has determined that. You can't leave when there's so much at stake and wolves are being attacked."

"You're more important." He brushed his fingers along my cheek. "I'd rather do that than lose you."

"Dove is right," Rosemary said, making me cringe.

I was so damn tired of that name. "It's Sterlyn." She at

least deserved to know that after everything that went down.

"Thank God. Because Dove is a horrendous name." Rosemary groaned.

"It is not." Killian frowned. "I thought it was fitting because of her hair."

"Of *course* he gave you that name." Rosemary took her phone out of her pocket and then glared at Griffin. "With the wolf attacks, if you were to step down, it would cause anarchy, and you know it. The best thing we can do is figure out who's after Sterlyn and go from there."

"That crow is heading back to whoever wants her." Killian's hands clenched into fists. "And we're at a disadvantage, but I'm hoping we'll find something on the boat that can point us in the right direction."

"I've got to go, but are you working tomorrow?" Rosemary faced me.

There was no reason not to right now. If I didn't go in, things would look even more suspicious. "Yes, I am. We need to pretend everything is as normal as possible after the shit show today."

"I agree." She nodded. "I'll run by and talk to you then. I've got to get back to Shadow City—Mom is looking for me." She hurried out the door and took to the sky.

Griffin pursed his lips. "Was it me, or was it like we weren't even in the room?"

"Get used to it." Killian pointed at me. "Ever since she came into my life, I'm the chauffeur."

That was kind of true. "As fun as this is, I'm going to head outside and help the others."

"Nope, you're not." Griffin pulled me into his arms. "They have enough people, and they know what they're doing. After almost dying, I'd like to take you on that date."

"I don't feel like going out." I'd been so excited earlier about spending time with him, but between what we'd gone through and my subpar outfit, all I wanted to do was crawl into bed.

"Then you two go over to Griffin's and chill while I go help the others." Killian gestured to the door. "Between you getting injured and Griffin almost dying, I say you've done enough today. Besides, I'm thinking it's time that both Griffin and I start stepping up to our responsibilities."

In other words, it was time to be the alphas they were destined to be.

"He's right." Griffin started to pull me toward the back door.

Unable to say no, I nodded but stopped in front of the man I viewed as my brother now. "Are you sure you don't need me there? I don't mind helping."

"I know." He booped my nose. "But I want you to get to know him—the side of him that I know. I'm giving you my seal of approval."

"With the womanizer?" I asked and pointed at Griffin.

"Hey," Griffin growled.

"He took a bullet for you," Killian said as he opened the back door, waving us out. "I figure if that doesn't prove he meant what he said, nothing will."

The truth of his words made my heart pound, and I turned to face the sexy man who now held my heart. My wolf howled, and my body warmed, leading to the scent of arousal wafting off me. I locked eyes with my mate. "No more waiting." I'd had enough. I got that he wanted to do things right, but I needed him. And now.

"Oh, dear God." Killian shut the door and headed to the trees. "That's my cue to go."

A smirk fixed on Griffin's face as he led me toward his

home. Within seconds, we were entering his kitchen. I had no idea what the room looked like, and I didn't care. He slammed the door shut, and I slammed my lips on his.

He growled as he grabbed my ass and I wrapped my legs around his waist. The feel of his hands and mouth on me made both my body and wolf go wild.

I wrapped my arms around his neck, fisting his hair. He stumbled down the hall. In my half-lucid state, I realized his house was exactly the same floor plan as Killian's.

We entered the master bedroom, and he kicked the door shut behind us then tossed me on the bed. The cool blue of the walls was the shade of the ocean. I ran my hands over light muted gray sheets that reminded me of the sky on an overcast day.

But when Griffin stood over me, my eyes saw only him. He stared back at me, his hazel eyes glowing, and removed his shirt. His abs looked even more muscular than I'd imagined as they bunched and coiled. He leaned over me, trapping me between his arms.

"You're so beautiful," he said, sounding raw.

My breath caught as he kissed me, and his fingers pressed into my sides, turning me on even more. "You're not too bad yourself."

"Not too bad, huh?" He chuckled as his lips pressed against my throat and his hand lifted my shirt. "You've seen more handsome?"

"Define handsome," I teased as he unfastened my bra and removed both it and my shirt from my body.

Then I tensed, realizing we had one more thing to discuss.

"Stop." He froze, and I smiled to reassure him. I hated to interrupt our moment, but before we did this, we had to make sure we were on the same page. Normally, when fated mates completed their connection, they linked to the strongest wolf's pack. If the pair were two alphas, the packs remained separate unless the two alphas agreed to merge with only the fated mate bond linking the mates. But since I didn't have a pack, that meant I'd be linked with his...unless I purposely put up a barrier. "I want to complete our bond, but I can't submit to you and become one of your pack." I hoped that didn't anger him, but it was better to have this conversation beforehand. My wolf wouldn't submit to him, and even if she could, the rest of his pack would realize that I was different. My secret wasn't ready to be revealed.

At least, not yet.

"I want you any way I can have you. My goal isn't to be your alpha." He kissed my lips sweetly. "I'm all-in. Nothing will change that."

My stomach fluttered at his words, and somehow, my desire for him grew even stronger.

When his mouth captured my nipple, pleasure like I'd never experienced before waved through my body. I gasped as my fingers dug into his strong, muscular back.

My head swam from his unique scent and the hand he trailed slowly down my body. I'd never been touched this way, and I never wanted him to stop.

Slipping my hand between our bodies, I unbuttoned his jeans, needing to feel all of him.

"I'm trying to take care of you." He sighed, his breath hot against my skin.

But the problem was I *needed* him. "Slow can come later." The *tug* inside me was desperate—he had to make me whole and now. "Please."

"Fine." He stood up and removed my yoga pants and panties. "But we *are* going slow next time." He groaned as he scanned my body and removed the rest of his clothes.

He was even more delectable than I'd ever imagined. His body was hard in all the right places, and I did mean all.

He slipped his hands between my legs and rubbed.

My breathing caught as waves of pleasure gripped me. My body convulsed as he slipped his fingers inside.

With each movement, he had flames licking my body. "Oh, God," I cried out, about to lose my mind.

His tongue circled one breast and flicked over my nipple, causing sensations to shoot through me and bring me dangerously to the edge. I pushed him back and flipped us around, needing to take control. He was dominating me, and I loved it, but it was my turn. I straddled him and started to slip him slowly inside me.

"Whoa... wait." His irises glowed even more as he stilled. "You're—are you...?"

I writhed and started to press down, but his hands on my waist stopped me. "Am I *what*?" But then I realized what he meant, and my cheeks flushed hot.

"You're a virgin. We need—"

"No, I need *you*." My wolf howled. We'd waited long enough. I slipped him inside, filling me, causing the connection between us to grow.

"Wait," he rasped as he scooted us both to the headboard and propped himself up. His hands caressed my breasts as I began to ride him. Each time, he filled me more, going deeper and deeper.

Moving faster, he soon bucked underneath me, and my wolf surged forward, needing to cement the bond between us. My mouth went to his neck, and my teeth raked his skin, but I didn't want to completely break it until he gave me permission to claim him.

"Do it," he groaned. "Please."

That was all I needed to hear. My teeth broke his skin,

and his blood seeped onto my tongue while a part of my soul reached out and slammed into him.

"My turn," he growled, and I tilted my head willingly, offering my neck.

"Yes," I sighed, giving him my consent.

When his teeth entered me, his feelings and emotions collided with mine.

If I'd had any doubts about how he felt about me before, they were gone. All he saw was me, and he'd lay down his life to protect me again without a moment's hesitation.

My heart grew warm once more now that I wasn't alone, and my wolf put up a barrier to prevent the further pack connection.

Pleasure built within our bodies, and soon, orgasms ripped through both of us, our pleasure molding us into one.

Something snapped inside our chests, and our connection strengthened as our emotions poured into one another. Love merged us into one being, warming my chest and filling the space that had been cold for all too long.

I don't deserve you, Griffin linked.

His voice in my head caused happiness to surge through me. *No, you don't,* I teased. *And yet, you still have me.* I kissed his lips, so happy to be in his arms.

Completely exhausted and satiated, I rolled onto my side, and he pulled me into his strong, comforting arms. His fingers brushed my arm, up and down, and soon, I was out cold.

If I'd thought walking into Shadow Ridge University with Killian had been strange, this was a whole different matter.

Everyone we passed turned and stared as Griffin, the alpha of Shadow City, held my hand and walked me into the coffee shop.

Of course, it didn't help that as of yesterday, I'd been *dating* his best friend.

As we walked past the long coffee line, Carter's mouth dropped open, and he pointed from Griffin to me. "What the hell, Dove? I can't figure out if I'm impressed or disgusted. Weren't you with Killian yesterday?"

A growl emanated from Griffin's chest.

Behave. I understood comments like these weren't fun for Griffin, but we'd both known this would happen. "Killian and I were more friends than anything."

"With friends like that--"

Griffin snarled. *I never have liked him anyway. I may kill him.*

I laughed, not able to conceal my happiness.

"Stop," I warned Carter. "He's my fated mate. He's not enjoying your commentary."

"*What?*" he said loudly, causing the entire coffee shop to go silent. "Griffin completed the mate bond with you?"

"Yes." Griffin stepped in front of me and glanced at each person in line. "She is my mate, officially, in all ways. No hitting on her, and no hitting on me."

Well, that was pretty much equivalent to him peeing on me, but at least he'd included himself in that equation.

A few girls pouted, riling my wolf, but I pushed her down. There was no reason to let her get too worked up. If anyone tried something stupid, we'd kill them. Easy-peasy.

I hate to do this, but I've got to go to Political History and then International Relations. He kissed me a little longer than necessary. *I'll be back when classes are over.*

I'll be counting the seconds. I pulled away and gave him a smile.

He licked his lips and winked before walking out of the cafe while I enjoyed the view.

"Uh... Earth to Dove." Carter pulled me back into the present. "That cash register won't work itself."

I turned around and got to work.

A COUPLE of hours later when the line finally calmed down, Carter tapped my shoulder. "Hey, do you mind going into the back and getting more Italian roast beans? We're running low."

"Oh, yeah, sure." Usually, another co-worker got the beans because I was always so busy at the register, but Susan was on break. I remembered seeing the Italian roast when Carter showed me around the first day I started working here.

I walked past the kitchen to the small hallway closet next to the exterior door that led to the alley where they kept that smelly dumpster. I opened the storage door and started glancing through the inventory.

"That's weird," I whispered to myself. "It was on this shelf the last time I saw it." The third shelf held some of the dark roasts but not the Italian.

I had just squatted to check the bottom shelf when I heard footsteps coming my way. Carter must have needed something else or wondered what was taking me so long.

"Hey, Carter. Did you move the Italian roast? It's not on the top shelf," I asked, searching the labels near the floor.

I felt the hairs raise on the back of my neck as he stepped behind me, and then something sharp stuck into my neck, right above my collarbone. A familiar voice I couldn't quite place whispered, "I'm so sorry."

I tried to turn around, but the world began to spin.

My vision turned hazy, and all I managed to do was link to Griffin. *Help.*

ABOUT THE AUTHOR

Jen L. Grey is a *USA Today* Bestselling Author who writes Paranormal Romance, Urban Fantasy, and Fantasy genres.

Jen lives in Tennessee with her husband, two daughters, and two miniature Australian Shepherd. Before she began writing, she was an avid reader and enjoyed being involved in the indie community. Her love for books eventually led her to writing. For more information, please visit her website and sign up for her newsletter.

Check out my future projects and book signing events at my website.
www.jenlgrey.com

ALSO BY JEN L. GREY

Shadow City: The Silver Wolf

Broken Mate

Rising Darkness

Silver Moon

The Hidden King Trilogy

Dragon Mate

Dragon Heir

Dragon Queen

The Wolf Born Trilogy

Hidden Mate

Blood Secrets

Awakened Magic

The Marked Wolf Trilogy

Moon Kissed

Chosen Wolf

Broken Curse

Wolf Moon Academy Trilogy

Shadow Mate

Blood Legacy

Kingdom of Fire

The Pearson Prophecy

Dawning Ascent

Enlightened Ascent

Reigning Ascent

Stand Alones

Death's Angel

Rising Alpha

Made in the USA
Las Vegas, NV
19 June 2022

50438786R00152